THE ECCENTRIC MISS DELANEY

THE ECCENTRIC MISS DELANEY

Gail Mallin

CHIVERS

British Library Cataloguing in Publication Data available

This Large Print edition published by BBC Audiobooks Ltd, Bath, 2007.
Published by arrangement with the author.

U.K. Hardcover ISBN 978 1 405 64138 8
U.K. Softcover ISBN 978 1 405 64139 5

Printed and bound in Great Britain by
Antony Rowe Ltd., Chippenham, Wiltshire

CHAPTER ONE

'Ostler! Ostler!' The deep voice rang round the inn yard.

Jethro came running but halted in awe as the sporting curricle came to a precision halt in the centre of the Peacock's modest yard. It had a glossy yellow body and was drawn by a high-stepping pair of match-bays. To add to his astonishment, it was being tooled by one whom even he recognised as a Nonpareil.

Nick Verlaine sighed. He should have waited until he had reached Barton Grange but the fact that this little wayside tavern lay on the outskirts of the modestly fashionable resort of Parkgate had encouraged him to hope that it might offer better service than that usually found in such places. Still, beggars could not be choosers and he had a thirst on him that would brook no further delay.

'Look lively now, lad,' he encouraged the undersized youth who was still standing there, scratching his head in disbelief.

'Yes, sir.' Released from his trance by the note of impatience in this unusual customer's baritone tones, Jethro leapt forward to take joyful charge of the most wonderful horses he had seen in a twelvemonth.

Lord Verlaine sprang down with an athletic grace that belied the hours he had spent on the

1

road, and Jethro enviously noted his height. Six feet at least, aye, and broad-shouldered to match, he'd be bound, though that many-caped Benjamin made it difficult to be sure.

After giving his long limbs a stretch Nick strolled off in the direction of the taproom. To his surprise, it was impeccably clean and furnished with more comfort than the modest exterior of the building had seemed to promise. His black brows rose a further fraction of an inch when he perceived that instead of a tapster there was a dumpy middle-aged woman presiding over the tankards.

'Good afternoon, sir.'

Her voice was as genteel as her dowdy dress of brown kerseymere. For an instant Nick wondered what the devil this image of respectability was doing in such queer employment, but abandoned his curiosity when she handed him the tankard of cool ale he had been craving this hour past.

'My compliments, ma'am. An excellent brew!' His first thirst slaked, Nick called for another and while it was being poured became aware of the stir his entrance had caused. Mildly amused by the covert looks directed at him by a pair of farmers in stained smocks and the more frank stare from an ancient crouched in the inglenook, he concluded that the fashionably clad were not often met with on these premises.

'Begging your pardon, sir, but perhaps you

would prefer to sit in the coffee-room?' asked the woman with a quiet deference.

Curbing the impulse to retort that he had no intention of being stared out of countenance by a parcel of yokels, Nick nodded. The offer was meant well and although he did not think himself top-lofty it might grow wearisome to be the object of such abundant curiosity.

'Thank you. Where may I find it?' he asked.

'Step into the passage, sir, and it is the first door on your left. It will be empty, since all our guests are out at present.'

Nick proceeded to follow these directions but as he entered the long low room he saw that the proprietress was mistaken.

'Well, now, here's a hive of industry!'

At the sound of his voice her cheerful humming abruptly ceased and the girl spun round, affording him an excellent view of her enchanting countenance, framed by untidy but glossily blue-black curls spilling from a frayed ribbon.

Nick whistled softly. Replace that shabby gown and apron with some fashionable frippery and this wench would give the beauties of Almack's a run for their money! He'd never seen eyes more blue . . . or a more kissable mouth.

'Don't you find it too warm a day for such work?' he enquired, abandoning his tankard upon a table and striding forward.

'Cleaning is required at all times of the year.'

Neither the coolness of this curt answer nor the surprisingly cultivated tones in which it was delivered registered with Nick. His attention was far too taken up with admiring her figure. She was a little on the tall side perhaps, but so exquisitely proportioned that he wouldn't cavil at that!

One shining black ringlet had strayed across her lusciously full bosom. Nick raised his quizzing-glass. Damn it, but she'd skin like satin! So smooth and creamy white that it made his fingers fairly itch to reach out and stroke it.

A bloom of colour stained the beauty's cheeks.

'Did you require anything in particular, sir?' she enquired in a tight little voice, laying down her duster.

A mischievous smile lit Nick's eyes.

'Only this,' he replied, sweeping her into his arms with a speed and efficiency born of long practice.

Before she could recover from her astonishment at being handled in such a fashion, Athena Delaney found herself being thoroughly kissed.

'Oh, how dare you behave in such a way?' she exclaimed the instant his lips left her own. Struggling to free herself from a stronger hold than she had ever known, she added hotly, 'Let me go at once.'

The steely arms merely tightened their grip. 'Not unless you give me another kiss first,' Nick laughed.

'Give!' Athena's angry voice rose in protest. 'A strange notion you have, sir, of giving. I'd as lief give you the plague!'

'You little firebrand,' Nick said admiringly. 'Tell you what, I'll trade you a guinea for it.'

If she had not been quite so crushed against his chest, Athena's bosom would have undoubtedly swelled, but a strangled shriek left Nick in no doubt of her indignation.

'Come now, am I as repulsive as all that?' he demanded with a grin.

'You, sir, are entirely repugnant,' Athena spat at him, not entirely truthfully, for it had not escaped her notice even in these trying circumstances that he was a very handsome man, if one had a fancy to swarthy looks, which she did not, of course. 'But that is hardly the point—'

'You're not going to tell me that other customers haven't tried to steal a kiss or two before now,' he interrupted in a wondering tone.

A furious nod of her raven head answered him.

'What, never? You must be bamming me, or else they are such a set of slowtops here on the Wirral as I have never encountered before in all my life!'

Nick's expression was ludicrously droll and for an instant, insanely, Athena was tempted to smile back at him, but she had no intention of encouraging his effrontery.

Instead she said with all the severity she could muster, 'Pray release me and be done with this nonsense. Or I shall be forced to scream for help.'

'Ah, that does put a different complexion on it! Will you shout for that looby in the stables, I wonder? I declare I'm quaking in my boots.'

'Will you be serious?' Athena squirmed wildly in his embrace, infuriated by the teasing note in his voice, a deep voice she might have found pleasingly velvet-toned in any other man.

'Oh, I am serious, my beauty.' His arms tightened about her. 'Hold still! I intend to have that kiss come what may.'

There was a devilish light glinting in his dark eyes and Athena suppressed a shiver. He was as swarthy as a Spanish brigand with his black hair and tanned skin and instinctively she felt sure he was equally ruthless.

'You are mad, quite mad—' she began, but her protest was cut off abruptly as his lips captured hers once more.

A strange tingling filled Athena's limbs, and, although her brain was instructing her to fight him, foolishly she could not comply. Her body seemed to have acquired a will of its own and moulded itself pliantly to the hard contours of his frame. Incredibly, instead of trying to pummel his shoulders, her fists uncurled to clutch him eagerly to her. Even more horrifyingly, obeying the warm skilful pressure of his mouth, her tightly closed lips parted in invitation.

Her senses swimming, Athena was scarcely aware at first that he had finally released her until he spoke.

'Name whatever price you wish, wench,' Lord Verlaine said hoarsely, still breathing hard. 'By God, it will be worth it!'

'You . . . you villain!' The exclamation was ripped from Athena's throat as her hand flew up to make explosive contact with his cheek.

Ruefully rubbing his sore face, Nick reflected on the folly of relaxing one's guard before making certain of victory. 'There's no need to look such daggers at me, girl. I can take a hint!'

'My virtue is not for sale.' Athena spoke through clenched teeth.

'Obviously,' Nick drawled, leaning back to prop his lean hips against the nearest table. He surveyed her with a faint smile as he folded his arms across his chest. 'My luck must be out. I encounter the prettiest chambermaid in England, only to find she is virtuous to boot. What a curst pity!'

Athena's Celtic blue eyes widened. 'You . . . you think me a chambermaid?'

He directed a silent glance over her untidy

7

hair and faded dimity gown that spoke more eloquently than words.

Taking a deep breath, Athena strove to control her temper. 'You are mistaken, sir. My name is Delaney and since my ancestors were once kings in Ireland I dare say my birth is as good as yours.'

'Then what the devil do you mean by dressing up in that rig?' Nick retorted. 'Good God, what did you expect me to take you for?'

'Oh, I see, you would not have molested me if you had known my quality?'

Her sarcasm brought an unaccustomed tinge of colour into his tanned cheeks. 'I play by the rules, Miss Delaney,' he growled.

'And chambermaids are fair game, are they not, for men of your stamp?' She sniffed disdainfully.

Nick coughed and fingered his neckcloth as if the Trône d'Amour he had tied that morning had suddenly become too tight. 'What can your people be thinking of,' he exclaimed gruffly, 'letting you run loose in such a manner with not even a maid in attendance?'

'There is nothing in *my* behaviour to cause the least distress to anyone,' Athena declared. 'And I'll have you know that I do have a chaperon.'

Comprehension dawned in Nick's dark eyes. 'Do you mean that dowdy, bracket-faced female in the taproom?' he demanded

8

incredulously.

'Sherry is not bracket-faced! She has a great deal of countenance,' Athena fired up in passionate defence of her beloved former governess.

He grinned at her. 'Doing it rather too brown, Miss Delaney.'

'Your opinion, sir, does not concern me in the least!' Athena sought refuge in dignity. 'What does signify, however, is that you had no business to pounce on me in that odious manner and if you were a gentleman you would apologise instantly.'

His grin broadened, revealing excellent white teeth. 'I haven't the least intention of apologising for something I enjoyed a great deal.' He paused significantly. 'What's more, unless I'm very much mistaken, you enjoyed it too. At least on the second occasion,' he added fairly.

'Oh, you are . . .' Athena blushed furiously.

'Impertinent?' he supplied helpfully, as she struggled for words.

'An outrageous coxcomb!' she snapped back.

'No doubt, ma'am, but you must shoulder some blame for my behaviour. I would never have acted in such a manner if you had not been dressed like a servant—'

'Would you have me wear a ballgown to wield a duster? Pray, do not be ridiculous,' Athena interrupted.

9

'The only absurdity, ma'am, lies in finding a lady of your quality engaged in such a menial occupation,' he retorted swiftly.

Athena's beautifully shaped mouth thinned to a narrow line, a sure sign of temper, as any of her friends could have informed Lord Verlaine.

'I'm not surprised a blockhead like yourself should think such old-fashioned, fustian nonsense,' she replied scornfully. 'There is no shame attached to honest work, my buck! Why should I not dust this room, pray, when I own a share in the inn?'

Nick gazed at her blankly, and, taking advantage of his astonishment, Athena went on coolly, 'And now I'll thank you to leave, sir. I have work to do even if you have not!'

For an instant Nick was inclined to dispute the matter but common sense, to say nothing of previous experience in dealing with females wearing just that determined expression, warned him it would not serve.

'As you wish, Miss Delaney.' He bowed with exquisite grace and headed for the door, where he paused, his hand on the handle. 'But I'll be back.'

*   *   *

Barton Grange lay on the north-western extremity of the Wirral peninsula. Enclosed by lush acres of parkland, the original black and white half-timbered Tudor hall had been much enlarged and improved upon by subsequent generations of the Barton family.

The improvements included a handsome library in the west wing and it was to this apartment that the present incumbent, a stoutish, fair-haired gentleman in his mid-thirties, led his guest once Lord Verlaine had rid his person of the dust of the road.

'Try some of this Madeira,' Sir George offered genially, directing his friend to the most comfortable chair with one expansive wave of his hand.

'Thank you, I will.' Nick accepted the proffered glass. 'I have need of it.'

A wide grin split George's round face. 'I know, I know. Why must I live beyond the reach of civilisation? Family obligation, dear boy. I durst not sell the place. Only think of what my mother would say!'

Nick, who had the doubtful privilege of being acquainted with the Dowager Lady Barton, acknowledged this remark with a smile, but his darkly handsome face sobered as he murmured absently, 'I wasn't thinking of the journey.'

'Don't leave me in suspense, dear boy,' his former comrade in arms begged, as Lord Verlaine fell into a brooding silence.

Thus admonished, Nick apologised for his lapse of manners and related the events that had taken place earlier. All he left out was any

11

mention of his second attempt to kiss the lady. For some strange reason, he could not rid himself of the marvellous feel of her, so soft and willing in his arms. He strongly suspected her wonderfully wanton response had amazed her almost as much as it had surprised him, but he did not want to talk about it, even to so good a friend as Sir George.

'I might have known there'd be a petticoat in it,' George chuckled. 'There always is with you!'

Nick shrugged wryly. 'Ah, but this time I didn't even manage to find out the lady's given name.'

'Athena,' replied Sir George promptly.

'You know her?' Nick's gaze sharpened.

'Oh, everyone hereabouts knows of the eccentric Miss Delaney!' George grinned. 'You're not the first to be smitten by those glorious eyes, you know. Half the fellows in the county fancy themselves in love with her, but the devil of it is that she's a confirmed man-hater.'

Nick's eyebrows soared.

'It's true.' George gave his fair head a solemn shake. 'A great pity, but there it is. Says she won't get married. Got some crazy notion in her head of making her own fortune on the 'Change.'

'Gammon.' Nick snorted derisively. 'Females don't speculate.'

George spread his hands in a doubtful

12

gesture. 'Thought so too myself until I met Miss Delaney,' he admitted, 'but she's been devilishly successful according to William Taylor.'

Seeing Nick's look of enquiry, he explained that this gentleman was the owner of the area's most influential banking house. 'He's been advising her on her investments. Knows about the latest ships leaving Liverpool and all that sort of thing.' A faint sigh escaped his lips. 'Dare say he'll succeed in winning her in the end. Respectable fellow, well-blunted, just the steady sort of man females fancy.'

On this depressing note he rose to pour them more wine.

'That's all very well,' said Nick, impatiently dismissing the worthy Mr Taylor. 'But what in hell's name is a girl like that doing at the Peacock?'

Sir George rubbed the side of his nose with a reflective finger. 'Can't rightly say. What I do know is that since she arrived at the Peacock last February with that female dragon in tow the place has changed out of all recognition.'

A discreet knock at the door heralding the arrival of Sir George's butler with the announcement that dinner was served prevented Nick from making a reply. Over an excellent meal of fillets of turbot, roast duck with French beans and mushrooms, mutton chops and a Chantilly basket contrived to tempt Sir George's sweet tooth, he confined

13

himself to safely neutral topics of conversation, but once the servants had withdrawn and they were left alone to enjoy their port he immediately returned to the fascinating subject of Miss Delaney.

'Do you think it's true that she comes from a good family as she claimed?'

'Oh, aye,' George confirmed. 'Her grandfather is old General Sir Patrick Delaney.'

Nick whistled. This gentleman's exploits in the late war with the Colonies were well known to all military men.

'Say, do you ever regret selling out after Waterloo, Nick?' George demanded suddenly, his thoughts turning to his own recent career. 'I know I do sometimes.'

'Sapskull,' Nick retorted affectionately. 'You'd hate to serve in peacetime.'

'I suppose so,' his friend sighed. 'But we did have some good times in the Peninsula and civilian life can be so damned boring!' He glanced slyly at Nick. 'I swear that's the reason you began kicking up larks all over Town.'

Nick shrugged, unwilling to consider the matter. His former life as a Major in the 5th Dragoon Guards was in sharp contrast to his present idle existence, a fact he tried hard to forget. Lack of purpose since quitting the Army had made him restless, and his efforts to solace his boredom with deep drinking, heavy gambling and a series of dazzling mistresses had earned him a dashing reputation but no inner peace.

'We ain't discussing my affairs,' he said firmly, 'but Miss Delaney's.'

'Ho, ho, so that's how the land lies, is it?' George exclaimed. 'You'll catch cold at the game, Nick. She ain't keen on rackety fellows, I warn you.'

'Then how did you come to meet her?' his friend enquired sweetly.

George grinned. 'Harmless as a newborn lamb, that's me,' he declared.

Nick snorted rudely, but his threat to repeat several warm stories to refute this claim was averted by George hastily embarking on a recital of his first meeting with Miss Delaney at the Assembly House in Parkgate.

'She is received, then?' Nick asked in a carefully uninterested tone.

'Oh, lord, yes. Parkgate ain't one of your stuffy resorts like Worthing. She dances divinely, too.' George chuckled reminiscently. 'Course, some of the tabbies objected on account of her doings at the Peacock but nobody took any notice of their spite, I can tell you, least of all Athena. She don't give a fig for the gossip about her.'

He paused to offer his guest a cigarillo, a habit he had acquired while in the Peninsula. Nick declined but waited politely until it was lit and George had settled himself comfortably back into his chair before resuming the conversation.

'So, in your opinion, Miss Delaney is no shrinking violet,' Nick remarked thoughtfully.

George gave a shout of laughter. 'Not she! Up to snuff if ever I saw one. I've seen her dampen the pretensions of more than one hopeful buck with just a haughty look.'

An impish grin suddenly appeared on his cherubic countenance. 'Mind you, none of them could claim your polished address. Wonder if you'd fare any better?' He began to chuckle. 'Lord, I'd give a pony to see you succeed in storming that citadel!'

'Is that a challenge, George?' Nick murmured softly. For once there was a glint of something other than boredom in his dark eyes.

'Aye, damme, why not?' His host's face shone with enthusiasm. 'That fascinating little witch has broken more hearts than I can count. It is time someone struck a blow for our sex. Come on, Nick, say you'll do it!'

Lord Verlaine remained silent for a moment, staring into the heart of his wine glass and remembering the scorn in those great sapphire eyes. She had dismissed him as though he was of no import and it still rankled!

Nick knew it was merely his vanity that had been hurt—he had grown too accustomed to easy conquests—but there was something irresistible about the idea of teaching Miss Delaney a lesson.

16

He lifted his dark head and saw that George was watching him eagerly.

'Done! A pony it is, then.'

Sir George let out a crow of triumph and raised his glass. 'Let's have a toast to your success,' he cried. 'What shall it be?'

Lord Verlaine raised his eyebrows. 'To the surrender of the citadel, what else?'

*　　*　　*

'Is the fish not to your liking, my dear? You've scarcely touched a mouthful.'

Athena Delaney jumped guiltily. Her mind had not been on her supper but the extraordinary event that had taken place earlier. In fact, she hadn't been able to stop thinking about it or the tall, swarthy stranger who had forced his way into her peaceful life!

She had been kissed before, of course. After all, she wasn't some green miss of seventeen; she was almost twenty-two years old and without being vain knew she was attractive to men. Their protestations of love and desire had never affected her cool judgement and it had not been in the least bit difficult to hold them off.

So what on earth had possessed her this afternoon?

He was very handsome, a little inner voice reminded her.

Yes, but I have known several men just as

17

good-looking and never given them a second thought, so that cannot be the reason, she answered herself quickly.

This reflection did not cheer her, and, failing to solve the mystery, she turned her attention to silently scolding herself for her shameless behaviour.

Any normal, well-bred girl would have fainted or fled, but I stayed to bandy words with him!

'Athena? Is there something wrong?'

Her one-time governess's anxious voice finally penetrated her chaotic thoughts and Athena strove to put her idiocy out of her mind.

'No, I'm just a little tired, that's all, Sherry,' Athena prevaricated, pushing aside her plate.

'I knew it!' Miss Sherrington exclaimed. 'You have worn yourself out. I wish you had not persuaded me to let that wretched girl have leave of absence.'

'But her mother is ill and you know very well that Peggy is needed at home,' Athena laughingly protested.

'Perhaps, but my first duty is to you, my dear. You were not bred for this kind of work. What would your father say if he could see you now?'

Athena's lovely smile faded. 'Doubtless Papa would say it served me right for not going to stay with my godmother as he wished,' she answered in a brittle tone.

'I do wish you had not quarrelled with him,' Sherry sighed.

'Are you sorry you came to Parkgate?' Athena asked quickly. She stretched out a hand across the scrubbed pine table and laid it gently over the work-worn fingers of her friend. 'I did not mean to drag you into something you disliked.'

Miss Sherrington's expression softened and she gave Athena's hand an affectionate little squeeze. 'Foolish girl, for my own part I have no complaint! Indeed, I think my situation improved beyond all recognition. Trying to drum anything at all into the heads of those silly children was an impossibility, but if you had not turned up that day and suggested we set up house together I should still be teaching in that abominable school and hating every minute of it.'

'I could not have managed without you,' Athena replied. 'Tom would have been reluctant to let me stay here on my own.'

Miss Sherrington acknowledged this with a nod of her grey head. Tom Shaw, the innkeeper, was her brother-in-law. They had not kept in touch after her sister's death three years ago, but, knowing him for a warm-hearted man, if something of a rough diamond, she had tentatively proposed they seek refuge at the Peacock.

'It will be a convenient base from which we can decide on our next move,' Miss Delaney had said, accepting the suggestion with alacrity.

In the event, their future had resolved itself. Appalled to find the inn in a filthy, run-down state, they had turned their energies to restoring it to its former glory. Shaken out of the drunken lethargy which grief had plunged him into, Tom was so grateful for their efforts that he had begged them to stay and help him run the place.

It had not been Athena's original intention to remain at the Peacock, but Tom's entreaties soon persuaded her that it was an excellent idea. Renting a house would make deep inroads into her small sum of capital whereas living at the inn would provide them with a roof over their heads free of charge and leave more money available for her ambitious schemes.

However, they both knew the situation was most irregular.

'Really, my dear, this is no life for you!' Sherry burst out at last. 'Living in a tavern! Eating in the kitchen!' She waved an agitated hand around her. 'It may do for a middle-aged spinster but you are a young lady of excellent family. You ought to be enjoying yourself at parties and balls and all that the season has to offer.'

Her outburst fell on deaf ears.

Such dark eyes he had. They appeared almost black but when you got close enough, and heavens, she could have hardly got any closer, it could be seen that they were really an intense moss-green, like agates!

'Athena? Athena, are you listening to me?'

Jerked abruptly from her reverie, Athena flushed hotly.

What is the matter with me tonight? she thought crossly. I must stop thinking about that detestable man.

'I'm sorry, Sherry. What were you saying?'

Miss Sherrington, deciding her young friend was more tired than she had first thought, obligingly repeated her remarks.

'Oh, Sherry, I have done all those things and a dead bore I found it for the most part!' Athena exclaimed. 'As soon as I was old enough to put up my hair Papa insisted on taking me about with him.'

'But that was on the Continent, my dear. You have never enjoyed a London season.'

Athena shrugged this objection aside. 'I cannot see that it would be so very different. Whenever Papa was in funds he spent lavishly, you know. Heavens, when we were in Paris a couple of years ago I had more dresses than I could possibly wear even though we were out every evening!'

She stood up and began to gather together the dirty plates. 'Of course, when Papa's fortunes were reversed we had to dodge his creditors while pretending that nothing was wrong.' A rueful laugh shook her. 'You cannot

21

imagine how horrid a time we had of it in Italy. I was never so glad as when Papa decided to come home the year after Waterloo.'

She carried the dishes over to the big stone sink, saying over her shoulder as she did so, 'Unfortunately, time had not softened my grandfather's anger. He had not forgiven Papa for eloping with Maman, so our journey to Ireland was all a waste.'

'I never understood why the General was so set against your mother, God rest her soul!' Miss Sherrington shook her grey head. 'I know it was very wrong of Mr Delaney to act as he did, but he was only a young man at the time, and, after all, your mother was of good birth. She was the daughter of the Comte de Montargis!'

Athena returned to the table and sat down.

'That was the trouble!' she explained. 'Grandfather could not abide foreigners, you see. Papa told me once that he'd had a devil of a time persuading him to let him go on a Grand Tour in the first place. Perhaps if Maman had possessed a good dowry he might have forgiven her, but her branch of the family was a poor one.'

A faint frown creased Athena's brow. 'I dare say it didn't help smooth matters over that I looked like her, apart from my colouring, which I get from Papa.'

Miss Sherrington smiled. 'Indeed you do resemble her in many ways, my dear, but that's nothing to be ashamed of, whatever your grandfather may have told you.'

'Oh, yes, I know. Maman was a dear but her memory still rankled with the General. He seemed to blame her for Papa's gambling, of all things. As if Maman could have stopped it!'

She sighed philosophically.

'In the end, of course, we came away with nothing. Not that I blame Papa in the least. After so many unpleasant things had been said, what else could he do?'

A little shiver ran through Athena. 'I would not be beholden to that man for anything. He might be my grandfather but he is a miserable old curmudgeon.'

Since Miss Sherrington agreed whole-heartedly with this view she did not think it incumbent upon her to reprove her young companion but strove to direct the conversation back into its former channel.

'I appreciate that you might have had a surfeit of parties, but how on earth are you to find a suitable husband if you do not go into the right sort of company?'

'Oh, Sherry, you know I don't want a husband! I prefer to rely upon my own wits, thank you.'

'But your investments might fail,' Sherry wailed.

Athena's eyes began to sparkle in a militant fashion.

'Then I shall survive by using my own two

hands. I'm not afraid of hard work. I do not need a man to keep me. In fact, I do not see that I need a man at all!'

Detestably, the image of the tall stranger of that afternoon came flooding back once more to mock her defiant words.

'If I ever marry at all,' Athena continued grimly, determined to ignore the tricks her perverse memory was playing on her, 'I shall take care to choose a sensible, quiet-living man and not some charming rake like my papa!'

CHAPTER TWO

The sun was out the next morning, making the waters of the Dee estuary sparkle brighter than a diamond necklace. The sight lifted Athena's spirits as she let herself out of the inn and strolled down the lane.

Directly ahead of her stood the Custom House, but as it was still early there was no one about, and Athena halted for a moment, drinking in the cool breeze and relishing the peaceful view.

She had passed a disturbed night, which was unusual for her, and woken with a headache.

'Go and get a breath of fresh air while I cook breakfast,' Sherry had ordered.

Meekly acquiescing, Athena had offered to

24

make herself useful. 'I can call in Swifts while I am out and leave our order. It will save time later.'

Since the butcher's shop was situated not far distant, only in School Lane, Sherry approved this plan, merely admonishing Athena to wear her cloak.

'I know the weather has been astonishingly warm for October, but it cannot last and I don't want you catching a chill.'

Athena had not argued but now she threw the offending garment back and, closing her eyes, lifted her face up to the gentle warmth of the sun.

'Good morning,' said a deep voice.

Athena's eyes flew open and saw the tall stranger of her daydream sitting astride a handsome roan not a yard away. What was more, he was just as handsome as her memory painted him with his clear-cut features which might have been modelled by a sculptor of classical inclination.

'What are you doing here?' To her annoyance her voice came out as a squeak.

'Did I startle you? How inconsiderate of me! Do forgive me, Miss Delaney.' Lord Verlaine's tone was suitably apologetic but there was nothing humble in his expression. In fact, there was a hint of laughter in his dark eyes.

'There is nothing to forgive,' Athena replied tightly.

The shock of seeing him so unexpectedly was wearing off and an unworthy pang of regret that she was wearing her plainest cambric gown assailed her.

'It relieves my mind to hear you say so.'

Athena glared at him, longing to ask him what the devil he was doing here in Parkgate when she had imagined him miles away by now.

'I'm staying with Sir George Barton,' Nick said, almost as if he had read her mind. 'He's an old army friend of mine.'

'Indeed.' Athena hid her dismay with a cool indifference but she could not help thinking that Barton Grange was far too close. 'Then do not let me keep you from him.'

'Oh, George won't mind!' Nick said easily. 'He's too idle these days to ride before breakfast but he wouldn't begrudge me the pleasure of your charming company.'

The smile that accompanied this flattering remark was one of Nick's best.

'Well, I do,' Athena retorted bluntly, frantically ignoring the sudden thumping of her pulse. Really, it was a very engaging smile! 'I have an errand to perform and even if I hadn't I still wouldn't waste my time talking to you.'

Nick winced. Well, he had been warned!

'Wait! Won't you let me accompany you?' he asked, quickly dismounting as she turned to go.

'I have not the slightest inclination for your company, sir, and you must know why.' Athena spoke rapidly but her mouth felt dry.

'Then will you at least accept my apologies for yesterday?'

Illogically, Athena felt a spurt of irritation and was betrayed into exclaiming, 'But you said that you enjoyed kissing me . . . oh!' She blushed in confusion and fell silent, mentally cursing her idiocy.

Nick concealed a flicker of triumph. So she was not as indifferent as she was pretending! 'I am still of the same mind about that,' he admitted. 'What I do regret, however, is that I appear to have caused you distress and I am most heartily sorry for it.'

Athena hesitated. It was on the tip of her tongue to tell him to go away but it seemed churlish to reject his apology.

'Please. I promise to behave myself.'

His grin was infectious and Athena found herself laughing.

'You are quite absurd, sir.'

'Come, if we are going to be friends, you must call me by my name.' He bowed slightly. 'Nick Verlaine, at your service, ma'am!'

'Considering you are holding the reins of your horse you managed that with considerable grace, Mr Verlaine,' Athena said sweetly. 'I dare say you've had a lot of practice. However, I am not in the habit of bestowing my friendship at such short notice.'

'Actually, it's Lord Verlaine,' Nick said, falling into step beside her and ignoring this attempt to put him in his place.

'Am I to be impressed?' Athena could not resist the impulse to flash a saucy smile at him.

'Oh, I hope so,' Nick murmured lazily.

Their eyes met and held for an instant before Athena looked quickly away.

'Tell me,' she continued a shade too brightly, 'is that coat one of Weston's? Papa always used to say he was the best tailor in London.'

'I hate to contradict any relative of yours but I prefer Scott.'

Recovering her poise, Athena nodded sagely. There had been something too intimate in his smile and it had thrown her. She would take care not to let it happen again.

'I have heard Scott is favoured by military men. You did say you were an army friend of Sir George's, did you not?'

Nick concurred smoothly, explaining that they had both served with Wellington in the Peninsula.

It did not surprise Athena to learn that he had been in the 5th Dragoon Guards. He had the splendid figure and erect bearing which was *de rigueur* for a cavalry officer and his seat on horseback was superb.

I wonder what he looked like in uniform? she thought curiously. He cut a handsome figure in his riding clothes but she suspected regimentals might suit him even better.

Suddenly realising that her musings were most indelicate, and entirely redundant besides, Athena hastily sought a safer topic of conversation.

Luckily, they had reached the part of the village where a sea-wall had been constructed to provide a promenade for visitors.

'This stretch is known as the Terrace,' she announced thankfully. 'All our fashionable visitors stroll here on fine afternoons.'

'Do you do so, Miss Delaney?' Nick asked at once.

'Oh, I do not count as a visitor!' Athena shook her head at him. 'I am here to earn my living.'

'Yet you are hardly a chambermaid,' he countered smoothly.

A tinge of colour crept into her face. 'You really must not refer to that deplorable incident.'

'So prim, Miss Delaney? Next you'll be telling me that I'm not to flirt with you either.'

There was such a twinkle in his agate eyes that Athena could not help laughing back at him.

'Have you no shame, sir?'

'None whatsoever,' he said promptly.

'Then you must be prepared to pay the penalty. No lady hereabouts will speak to you if you behave in such a scandalous manner.'

'You think they might not like it?' Nick

asked innocently.

Since Athena suspected that most of her acquaintance would like it only too well, she did not dare answer this!

'Not that it signifies,' Nick announced. 'I have no desire to pay court to any lady other than yourself.'

'Indeed, sir? How very rash, for I might give you the go-by and then where should you be?'

'Surely one so fair could not be so cruel!'

It was a long time since Athena had enjoyed this kind of flirtatious sparring; her current admirers spouted ponderous compliments that bored her to tears. Without meaning to, she found herself automatically responding in kind to Nick's teasing gallantry.

'Now let me see, do the scandalous attentions of a peer of the realm count as more flattering than those of a mere commoner?'

'Oh, definitely,' came the prompt answer.

'Then I must be careful you do not turn my head, must I not?'

'I could hope for no happier fate than to be allowed to try.'

Athena's eyes sparkled. 'I hate to cast a rub in your way but I feel I ought to point out that such hopes must be in vain. I am no green girl, you see.'

Nick smiled at her. 'Thank you for the warning—you may be sure I'll bear it in mind. Of course, I cannot promise not to flirt with you. You are too entirely beautiful for any man to resist.'

Athena coloured slightly. She had meant to be coolly distant and here she was encouraging him to make outrageous remarks!

Sherry is always telling me I am an incurable flirt, she thought dismally. Perhaps she is right!

A somewhat tense silence descended.

'Are those bathing machines down on the shore?' enquired Lord Verlaine lightly. He was too experienced a campaigner not to recognise her sudden discomfort and he had no intention of spoiling this promising beginning by rushing his fences.

Athena gladly turned her gaze to follow the direction of his. 'Yes but they are meant for the use of ladies only.'

'How can you tell?'

Thus prompted, Athena pointed out the modesty hood gracing each vehicle, which was meant to keep prying eyes at bay. 'The bathing woman also ensures that the horse has pulled the machine well into the water before she allows her customer to descend so that there is no chance that modesty may be offended. That would never do!'

'Have you tried this sea-water cure, Miss Delaney?'

'Only once,' Athena laughed. 'It was horridly uncomfortable. You have to wear the most voluminous gown made of stiff canvas

31

and if you do not meekly permit your bathing woman to duck you under the waves she all but drowns you in her attempts to do.'

Nick listened to her description with lazy enjoyment and so skilfully did he draw her out that Athena quite forgot her previous reservations and continued to chat to him in the most natural manner as they walked along.

'Oh, here we are already!' she exclaimed in some surprise as they drew level with the shop which was her destination. 'I must say goodbye now, my lord.'

Rather shyly she held out her hand.

Knowing he must not offend her by going too fast, Nick did not make the mistake of raising it to his lips but shook it politely.

Athena let out the breath she did not know she had been holding. Perhaps she had misjudged him and he could be trusted to behave as a gentleman ought. And yet . . .

'I have enjoyed our conversation, Miss Delaney. Perhaps you will do me the honour of letting me call upon you tomorrow?'

Athena's instincts prompted caution. His behaviour this morning had been exemplary but she wasn't such a fool as to plunge headlong into intimacy with a man she strongly suspected of being a rake.

'I'm afraid my commitments at the inn do not permit visitors, sir,' Athena replied demurely and noted his swift frown with a *frisson* of wicked enjoyment she could not quite suppress.

So, the little baggage was prepared to flirt with him, was she? But only on her terms, it seemed. We'll see about that, thought Nick to himself grimly.

'Then may I look forward to seeing you at the next Assembly? There is to be one on Thursday evening, I believe.'

'How clever of you to have found that out so quickly,' admired Miss Delaney. 'But I seldom attend at the Assembly House, I'm afraid.'

Keeping a tight hold on his temper, Nick tried another tack. 'But you will be going to the firework display, surely?'

Athena contemplated denying it but guessed that he had already discovered that this was to be the last big public event in Parkgate's season. Everyone would attend and both Sherry and Tom would think it very odd if she cried off.

'I may do so,' she murmured cautiously.

'Good.' Nick smiled at her but to her surprise he did not go on to offer his escort.

Since she had fully intended to turn him down had he suggested it, Athena could not understand her sense of disappointment and she watched him remount his horse feeling distinctly piqued.

My point, Miss Delaney, thought Nick with savage satisfaction as he caught a brief glimpse of her inner turmoil before she schooled her expression to bid him a polite farewell.

Lord Verlaine rode off and Athena lingered for a moment, watching him. However, as soon as she realised what she was doing she flushed and quickly turned away.

*   *   *

'Well, miss, you look right handsome tonight, that you do!' exclaimed the landlord of the Peacock as the fairytale vision that was Athena Delaney in an evening gown of sapphire silk floated into their private parlour.

'Why, thank you, Tom,' Athena replied, gratified by his reaction.

It had been so long since she had occasion to wear this particular gown that her reflection in the looking-glass in her tiny attic bedroom had surprised her. She had forgotten how the low-cut Russian bodice and tiny puffed sleeves suited her.

'Good gracious, child, you're never going to wear that, are you? You'll freeze to death!'

Miss Sherrington was staring at her in consternation. Her own stout figure was sensibly clad in grey bombazine, cut high at the neck and low on the wrists.

'But it is a lovely evening, Sherry,' Athena laughingly protested. 'And I mean to wear my blue velvet pelisse, so you mustn't worry.'

Sherry sniffed. She wasn't convinced but she knew that stubborn look of old so she contented herself with merely saying,

'Watching fireworks go off is a cold business. You would do well to forgo fashion in favour of a little comfort.'

Athena agreed soothingly.

The night sky was clear as they stepped out of the inn a few moments later.

'Signor Saxoni will have his work cut out to rival these stars,' Sherry remarked, looking up.

'Eh, watch where you are putting your foot, sister-in-law!' Tom exclaimed as she promptly stumbled. 'You'd best take my arm.'

Muttering about disgraceful pot-holes, Sherry accepted his assistance.

Tom then turned to Athena and asked her if she wanted the use of his other arm. Since he was much of a height with Sherry, and twice as stout, she knew that they would present an odd sight but she accepted, not wishing to hurt his feelings. When they had first arrived at the Peacock he had treated her with awe and although that initial awkwardness had worn off Athena knew he still considered her above his touch.

Tom's girth did not incline him to walk at speed so by the time they reached the shore beneath the Terrace it was crowded. With a sinking feeling, Athena saw that most of the forms set up on the sands were already taken.

'Let's try further along and see if we can find any free seats,' she suggested.

Her companions exchanged dubious glances.

'I doubt if there will be an inch of room anywhere, my dear,' Sherry said doubtfully. 'But we shall try it if you wish.'

After a few minutes jostling, Athena realised it was hopeless. Everyone seemed determined to struggle to the fore to claim a seat.

'Bother!' she exclaimed impatiently. For herself she did not mind standing in the least but she knew that neither of her companions would enjoy the spectacle if they had to remain on their feet.

Just then, Tom spotted a crony of his, who hailed him with an offer to squeeze up and fit them in.

Encouraged by her brother-in-law, Miss Sherrington sank down thankfully, but once Tom had taken his place next to her it became clear that there simply wasn't enough room for another person on the wooden bench.

'No, Tom, please do not get up,' Athena said swiftly, forestalling his attempt. 'You must remain with your friends.'

'Are you sure, miss?' He wavered in the face of this determination, feeling it was hardly his place to contradict her.

'Truly, I prefer to stand,' she insisted.

'I don't rightly know, it don't seem right. Shall I ask Sherry—?'

'Oh, there is no need! I will see you both later,' Athena murmured and slipped away before he could interrupt his sister-in-law's conversation with her neighbour on the other side.

The crowd thinned beyond the benches and Athena soon found a convenient place to watch the first rockets go up in a blaze of coloured light.

It wasn't until they had faded and the next group of fireworks were being set off that she became aware that she had acquired a considerable quantity of the beach in one dainty sandal and it was rubbing her foot.

'Sherry was right. I should have worn boots,' she muttered.

Since it was clearly impossible to hop up and down on one leg while trying to remove the offending particles, she decided to move further back and steady herself against the sea-wall before attempting the task of shaking them out.

'Sand in your slipper, Cinderella?'

Athena jumped in alarm and would have fallen over if a strong arm had not instantly appeared to hold her up.

'Must you keep sneaking up on me?' she exclaimed furiously.

Light showering down on them from an exploding rocket revealed the grin on Lord Verlaine's face as he released her. 'Sorry, ma'am.'

Athena was so incensed at being caught at such a disadvantage when she had meant to be so cool and elegant, if they did happen to meet, that she forgot to keep her unshod foot clear of the sand.

'Let me help,' he ordered. 'You are only making matters worse.'

Taken by surprise, Athena found it was too late to object. He had her slender foot in a firm grip and was dusting off the sand.

His hand was warm and its heat penetrated her silk stocking. The movement of his long fingers was equally disturbing. She could feel the strength in them but she knew he was trying to be gentle. In fact, his touch was almost like a caress . . .

Involuntarily, Athena caught her breath and the tiny sound carried to Nick's keen ears in spite of the noise all around them.

He glanced up at her quickly. 'Did I hurt you?'

'No, not at all.' Athena strove to sound calm.

Nick slid the sandal back into place and straightened. 'There, you're done.'

'Thank you.' Athena tried to quell the absurd regret that flooded over her the instant he released her. Was she going insane?

Nick stared down at her, his gaze absorbing her lush beauty. He had been very tempted to sweep her into his arms and kiss her just now and only the thought that she must surely repulse him had stopped him.

He had been looking for her, of course, but he hadn't expected the crowd to be so great.

The whole town must have turned out. If she hadn't been standing in this lonely spot he would never have found her.

'Surely you did not venture out here alone?' Concern suddenly sharpened his voice.

'Of course not,' Athena snapped back.

He was standing very close. She had only to stretch out a hand and it would encounter the fine cloth of his coat. Giddiness swept over her as she realised that was exactly what she wanted to do. She wanted to touch him!

Heavens, but she was behaving like an idiotic fool!

'Not that it is any of your business, but I came with friends,' she informed him tartly.

'Where are they? I'll take you back to them.'

'Oh, no, you won't!' Athena's nerves were so on edge that she bridled instantly. 'You have no authority over me, my lord. You may keep your odious masterfulness for those unfortunates in your employ. *I* have no intention of going anywhere with you.'

Nick took a deep breath. 'Look, I'm sorry if I offended you. I didn't mean to sound overbearing.'

'Well, you did.' Her retort sounded childish even to Athena's ears.

'Only because I'm concerned about your safety. You shouldn't be wandering around in the dark on your own,' Nick protested.

'Heavens, this is Parkgate, my lord, not London. What on earth do you suppose might happen to me?'

'You can meet rogues anywhere,' Nick affirmed doggedly.

'How true!' Athena's gaze raked him up and down.

Nick began to laugh. 'Well, I'll not quarrel with that!'

His good-natured acceptance of her gibe made Athena realise how bad-tempered she was being.

'I beg your pardon. That remark wasn't fair,' she admitted in a small voice. 'You have been most kind to me this evening.'

'Gammon!'

Her raven head came up with a jerk of surprise.

'Don't spout polite nonsense at me; I don't want that from you.' Nick hardly knew why he felt so angry. Didn't her conciliatory tone prove he was at last getting somewhere?

'I . . . I don't understand.' Athena felt bewildered by his sudden change of mood. 'What do you want from me?'

'Can't you guess?' he demanded savagely. 'No? Then take a look in your mirror, Miss Delaney.'

'Are you trying to warn me you are a rake, my lord?' Athena asked with more composure than she felt.

'Foolish of me, ain't it?'

Nick had regained control of himself. Damn it, why had he behaved like some canting

Puritan? He'd had her eating out of the palm of his hand. Now he'd blown his chance of winning George's wager for sure. Ten to one, she'd take fright and freeze him out before he could wangle an opportunity to rectify his mistake.

To his surprise, however, her lovely mouth twisted in wry amusement.

'Amazingly chivalrous, I would have said. I suppose I ought to be grateful.'

Nick's frown vanished at her light tone.

'You, Miss Delaney, are a flirt,' he said slowly.

'Then we are well matched, sir,' she answered serenely.

Lord Verlaine gave a shout of laughter but his mirth was suddenly drowned out in a burst of clapping and cheering from the crowd.

'I fancy the display must be concluded,' he said.

Athena saw people beginning to stand up and leave the benches. 'You are right, sir.'

'Won't you reconsider and let me escort you back to your companions?' Nick asked gently.

'I suppose I ought to hurry. Sherry will be having an apoplexy by now,' Athena replied evasively.

Dared she risk his company? He was too handsome for her good and he had admitted he was a rake but as she looked up into his smiling eyes Athena came to a decision. Caution be damned, she *wanted* to get to know him better!

'Very well, my lord. I will accept your escort but on one condition.'

Nick cocked his head at an enquiring angle. 'Which is?'

'That you don't tell Sherry about the sand in my shoe!' Athena laughed. 'Or I will never hear the end of it!'

*　　　*　　　*

'How goes the wooing, Nick?'

Lord Verlaine paused on the threshold of the breakfast parlour. 'Good God, George, don't you know better than to ask such questions at this hour?'

'I'll admit I ain't at my best so early in the day either but damme, man, you ain't hardly ever here. How else am I to find out?' Sir George protested.

'Later, dear friend, later!'

Nick strolled over to the sideboard where a lavish array of viands had been set out. Rejecting the covered silver dishes, he selected some cold beef and took his plate back to the table.

His host poured him a cup of coffee, knowing that Nick's taste did not run to ale at breakfast, and said with heavy sarcasm, 'Now are you ready to talk?'

Nick grinned at him. 'You know your trouble, George? You've got no patience.'

42

Then, seeing his friend's cherubic countenance begin to purple, he relented.

'Miss Delaney has accepted me as a suitable escort. I think she finds my company amusing.'

'So she should, by thunder!' George exclaimed, disappointed that Nick was not being more forthcoming. 'I've never known you dance attendance on a female like this before. I've scarcely seen you since that firework display the other week.'

He sounded distinctly miffed and his tone caused Nick to glance up at him in surprise.

'Blue-devilled, George?' he asked, laying down his knife and fork.

'Aye, well, but there's precious little fun to be had when you are forever off chasing that saucy little baggage.'

'Forgive me, I didn't realise I was neglecting my duties as your guest.' Nick's voice hardened.

'Now don't fly into a pucker, for God's sake,' George begged. 'Ignore my nonsense. I know very well that it was at my suggestion you started flirting with the wench so I can hardly cavil at your absence, can I?'

Nick scarcely heard this cheerful apology. He was too astounded by the wave of anger which had swept over him on hearing Athena described in such terms. For an instant he had wanted to knock George down!

It had been ten days since he had escorted Athena back to her friends and been introduced to them. Ten days and not one of them had gone by without him calling on her at the Peacock. They had strolled on the Terrace, taken a picnic on the Green and ridden together down winding country lanes. She had even stood up with him for one of the country dances at the Assembly House but most of all they had talked.

He had never known it was possible to enjoy a woman's conversation so much. Oh, he had flirted with innumerable pretty girls, relishing the cut and thrust of witty sparring and amorous innuendo. Sometimes he'd even found them capable of discussing serious matters in an intelligent way, but with Athena it was much more than that. It was though he had known her forever and could talk to her about anything!

It was an enlightening experience. From being merely the object of his desire, she had become a friend.

'I've got an idea. Why don't I ask her to pay a visit to the Grange?' George's face lit up as he made this suggestion. 'That way you won't have to go into Parkgate. Mind, we'll need a female to act as hostess. How about my mother?'

Nick raised his brows sardonically and George hastily amended his offer. 'Perhaps you're right, but we could ask someone else. My widowed cousin Emily would do, or better still your sister.'

'Of all the cork-brained notions, George!' Nick gave him an exasperated grin. 'Verena lives in London and has three children. She won't want to come posting up here at a moment's notice just to entertain a girl she hasn't even met.'

'She'd do it if you asked her. None of my relations are so devoted to my interests, let me tell you!'

Nick admitted that he was lucky. 'But I won't impose on Verena's good nature in such a shabby fashion,' he added firmly.

The baronet's expression became thoughtful. 'Well, how about my giving a ball, then?'

'It is very kind of you, but are you sure you wish to go to such effort?' Nick was dubious. Athena had declared her distaste for formal occasions, but long acquaintance with Sir George had taught him that his friend could be very persistent.

'Aye, why not?'

Lord Verlaine's attempt at tact was wasted. Sir George had the bit between his teeth.

'Damme, it's too long since I entertained and this is as good an excuse as any to enjoy a party.' He laughed heartily. 'Particularly as I stand to lose a pony if you win our wager.'

'Look, George, I think there is something you ought to know,' Nick said abruptly, but his friend wasn't listening.

'Champagne, that's what we'll need. I'd

45

better go and check the cellars with Butterworth. Don't want to run out halfway through the evening or people will be saying it is a shabby affair.' He jumped to his feet.

'George! About that wager; I want to—'

'Oh, don't worry your head about that, Nick!' said the baronet jovially as he hurried towards the door. 'I ain't bothered about the money.'

'Wait a minute, will you? George! It's not the money I want to talk to you about, you mutton-head! I want to call it off!'

But Lord Verlaine's voice fell upon empty air.

*   *   *

'Mr Taylor is here to see you, Miss Athena. I've put him in your private parlour.'

Peggy's greeting brought a little frown of dismay to Athena's wind-flushed face. She had just spent a delightful hour driving with Nick in his curricle and somehow she had no taste for William's sober company.

It is very remiss of me, she thought to herself as she thanked the chambermaid and slowly mounted the stairs, but it is all Lombard Street to a china orange that he will lecture me on the evils of frivolity!

Athena's forebodings proved to be accurate. There was a distinctly pettish look on William's long, narrow face as she entered the

46

room and his expression did not grow any warmer when she airily informed him she had been driving with Lord Verlaine.

'My word, Athena, I wonder at Miss Sherrington's allowing you to frequent that fellow's company.'

'Sherry is not the arbiter of my conduct, William.' Athena spoke quietly but there was a dangerous glitter in her Celtic eyes.

Seeing it, Mr Taylor, who was no fool, decided to moderate his sharp tone. 'I did not mean to imply any criticism of you, my dear. *Your* behaviour must always be ladylike, but I cannot trust that man. I have heard the most shocking reports of him. His reputation is a disgrace!'

'I didn't think you listened to tittle-tattle, William,' Athena replied cuttingly.

'It is my business to keep an ear to the ground,' Mr Taylor protested, a rather smug little smile turning up the corners of his thin mouth. 'Anyone who wishes to succeed in banking must know the weaknesses of his clients. They say Verlaine is a gamester as well as a rake. I should not like to touch his account.'

'I doubt if you will get the chance,' Athena retorted with poisonous sweetness.

'Athena, have I said something to upset you? I . . . I don't understand—'

'It is really very simple,' she interrupted. 'I know I have cause to be grateful to you,

William, but that does not give you the right to criticise my friends.'

'My dear, I have been most happy to help you with your investments! Surely, you realise I have only your well-being at heart?'

He looked so stricken that Athena's annoyance evaporated. 'You are all that is kind, sir. Now, perhaps we had better change the subject if we are not to quarrel.'

'Yes, yes, indeed.' He accepted this olive-branch with eagerness. 'I have been waiting for you to return so that I might talk to you about that copper mine you thought to invest in.' He smiled at her pacifically. 'It was doubly disappointing for me to find you out, you know, since I had been hoping you would visit me.'

Guiltily aware that she had half promised to do so, Athena obediently banished Lord Verlaine from her thoughts.

'Please, won't you sit down, sir? We can discuss the matter now if you wish.'

Folding his thin frame into a chair by the fireplace, William accepted her offer of refreshment. 'Some tea would be very pleasant. There is a distinct nip in the air, I find. I shouldn't wonder if this unseasonal spell is finally drawing to a close.'

'Oh, I hope not. It has been excellent for business,' Athena laughed, tugging the bell-pull to summon Peggy. 'I think we may even finish the year in profit.'

'Ah, it would be very gratifying to see this place paying its way once more. Such a satisfactory conclusion to all your hard labours!'

Athena agreed, wishing he would get to the point, but William did not like to be disturbed when dealing with financial matters and he waited until Peggy had taken their order and left the room before opening the discussion.

'Now I've had that fellow, Davis, investigated and I must tell you that I don't think it would be a wise move to invest in this mine.'

Gareth Davis had been one of their visitors earlier in the summer. Athena had liked the man and his eager desire to open his own copper mine in the Vale of Clwyd had aroused her sympathy. Seeing her interest, he had offered her the chance to throw her luck in with his.

'Why?' she enquired. 'The terms he offered were advantageous. I could reap a large return on my investment.'

'It is more likely that you would lose your money,' William answered. He handed her a closely written sheet. 'Here are the figures. Apparently, there is a problem with drainage. The engineers I have spoken to tell me that the mine is too wet to be profitable. I dare say Davis forgot to mention that little fact, eh?'

'Actually, he did tell me about it but he hopes to solve the difficulty with one of the new steam-engines.'

'Huh, then the man is a fool!' William snorted impatiently. 'It would be a ruinously expensive proceeding, from what I'm told. You would be well not to touch this scheme, my dear.'

Athena hesitated, giving the paper in her hand a second glance. In the past William's advice had been sound, but this particular matter lay outside his expertise and Gareth Davis's jaunty optimism had struck an answering chord within her.

'Perhaps you are right, William, but I think I will stick by my arrangement with Mr Davis,' she said quietly. 'Can you arrange for a transfer of funds?'

He frowned at her. 'I think you are making a mistake,' he warned, and for a moment Athena thought he was going to dispute her decision, but then he shrugged. 'However, if that is what you wish, I will put the matter in hand.'

She smiled her thanks at him, glad to avoid further argument.

Athena couldn't help wondering what had put him in such a bad mood. It wasn't like William to be so touchy. He had been a very good friend ever since she had asked him to handle her finances. Perhaps her inadvertent neglect had seemed discourteous?

A brisk knock interrupted her musing.

'Here is Peggy with our tea,' she murmured.

50

But the door opened to reveal Lord Verlaine.

'You dropped one of your gloves,' he informed her, strolling into the room with the lithe grace which was so characteristic of all his movements. 'I noticed it on my way back to the Grange.'

'How kind of you to return it so promptly.' Athena rose to her feet, instinctively smoothing the folds of her sprigged muslin skirts. She moved into the centre of the room to meet him, holding out her hand to take the lavender kid glove.

Nick's long fingers closed over hers. A little shiver went through her at his touch. 'Thank you,' she murmured, tilting her head to gaze up at him. The answering smile in his dark eyes set her pulse racing and she could not look away.

A loud cough from behind her recalled Athena to reality.

Flushing, she became aware that her hand still lay in Nick's warm clasp. Quickly disengaging herself, she turned to the banker, who had risen to his feet, and said in a creditably calm voice, 'I don't believe you have met Lord Verlaine, have you, William?'

He's a little older than I am, about thirty-four perhaps, Nick decided, as the introductions were performed. The banker was dressed quietly in grey, his eyes were also grey and his blond hair was fine and wispy, but there was nothing colourless in his expression.

A rival, unless I mistake my guess, Nick thought with a touch of amusement. If looks could kill!

'Do you intend to remain in Cheshire for long, my lord?'

The icy dislike in William's tone made Athena blink in astonishment.

'I haven't decided.' Nick flashed a glance at Athena. 'It all depends on the circumstances.'

William swallowed hard. 'I see,' he muttered.

Anxious to dispel the tension, Athena spoke up quickly. 'Lord Verlaine is staying with Sir George Barton, William. They served together in the Peninsula.'

'Indeed?' Mr Taylor's expression seemed to imply that the French had neglected their duty in overlooking this opportunity to dispatch his lordship.

'I fancy you are no admirer of the military, Mr Taylor,' Nick said smoothly.

'Most certainly not!' William glared at the taller man. 'I consider most soldiers to be little better than vagabonds. The recent war was a great waste of our resources, in my opinion. We would have done better to save our money and stay at home.'

A gasp of mortification escaped Athena but Nick's eyes twinkled with amusement at this vitriolic bluntness.

'I'm sure Bonaparte would have agreed with

you, sir,' he remarked sweetly and was rewarded by the dull flush that mottled the banker's thin cheeks.

Then, seeing Athena's embarrassment, he adroitly changed the subject. 'George is giving a ball in a few weeks' time. He plans to invite half the county, I believe. Dare we hope that you might be able to attend, Miss Delaney?'

'I should be delighted to do so,' Athena asserted, forgetting any reservations in a sudden burning desire to show Nick that she did not share William's ridiculous views.

'I think I had better take my leave,' Mr Taylor announced abruptly, realising she was angry with him.

'Yes, pray do so, William,' Athena agreed sharply.

Watching him depart, Nick knew he had made an enemy.

Just then Peggy arrived with the tray of tea.

'Will you stay, my lord?' Athena smiled at him in invitation.

'There's nothing I'd like better,' Nick replied, and promptly forgot about the banker.

CHAPTER THREE

Athena paused at the entrance of the Peacock's empty taproom where Peggy was busy sweeping the floor with a broom.

'Could you tell Sherry that I've gone to the Marine Library if she asks for me, please?'

The chambermaid looked up from her task and nodded, leaving Athena free to set off for the circulating library, which was situated at the seaward end of Drury Lane.

When she had first arrived Athena had thought it an odd coincidence to find so many Parkgate place-names the same as those in London, until Tom had explained to her that it had been a deliberate policy to make the village seem fashionable and so attract a better class of visitor.

Thinking about this reminded Athena that their remaining guests had departed that morning. Unfortunately, William's prediction concerning the weather had proved right. The lingering warmth of the last golden days of autumn had vanished and although the bigger inns such as the Princess Royal and the Boat House, which catered for ferry passengers sailing to Flint, might still be busy, the Peacock suddenly seemed deserted.

Well, it might be grey and windy but at least it isn't raining, Athena told herself stoutly. Yet even as she tried to imagine how pleasant it would be to have some time to herself after working so hard she was uneasily aware that winter would bring marked changes to the village.

As if to confirm her gloomy forebodings, the library was almost empty. A trio of ladies were scanning fashion magazines and an elderly gentleman stood reading the latest copy of the *Chester Chronicle* but Athena did not have to queue to change her books.

She was just about to leave when Lord Verlaine appeared.

He was looking very elegant in a blue coat of Bath suiting over a cream waistcoat and pale primrose pantaloons and Athena's pulse quickened. It was an effort to appear nonchalant as she said lightly, 'I did not expect to see you here, my lord.'

'Marble-backed novels hot from the Minerva Press are not my favourite reading,' he agreed with a teasing smile. 'However, I was told I could find you here, and what more promising lure could there be?'

A rosy blush coloured Athena's cheeks at his unexpected compliment and Nick promptly took advantage of it to relieve her of her basket and shepherd her outside.

'Shall we stroll along the beach?' he enquired, tucking her arm firmly into his.

'We should be blown away,' Athena laughed in protest.

'But I need a walk,' he retorted, adding with mock solemnity, 'Consider it an act of charity. George keeps too good a table!'

'If you desire exercise, you could try swimming.'

'No, thank you!'

'What, not even in the sea-water baths?'

Athena waved a hand towards a building they could see in the distance where the sea-wall ended. 'They have a warm bath, you know, for the convenience of valetudinarians.'

'Minx!' He grinned at her.

'Then we had better retrace our steps and essay the Cheltenham Walk if you are set on the idea of a stroll.'

'Where the devil is that?'

Athena explained that this sheltered promenade had been constructed as an alternative to the Terrace when the weather was rough. 'We can reach it if we go this way. It cuts across the far end of Drury Lane.'

Away from the houses the road soon assumed an air of rural tranquillity.

'Don't you find it too quiet?' Nick enquired, as the silence around them grew, broken only by birdsong and rustling autumn leaves.

'It is very restful.'

'So is the grave, my dear Miss Delaney!' Nick shook his head. 'The more I think about it the odder it seems.'

Puzzled, Athena tilted her chin enquiringly at him.

'Finding you here. You ought to be cutting a dash in Society.' He gave her an intent look. 'You have never told me the real reason.'

'But I did! I'm here to work,' she said, her expression innocent.

'Don't try to fob me off by telling me you enjoy playing innkeeper, my girl.'

56

'I wouldn't dare,' Athena replied meekly, but her eyes brimmed with laughter.

'I think you would dare anything.' Nick's tone was suddenly serious. 'It takes courage to defy the conventions and seek to control your own destiny.'

There was genuine admiration in his agate eyes and Athena felt a spurt of pleasure. 'I'm not so brave, sir,' she said, trying to hide her elation. 'It is merely that I did not care for the idea of being a companion or a governess and the only other respectable occupations open to women required skills I did not possess.'

He looked sceptical and she hurried on. 'Truly! I can sew a straight seam but I should never make a dressmaker or a milliner.'

'That doesn't explain what a girl of your breeding is doing slaving away in a little country tavern.'

Seeing he would not be fobbed off, Athena gave in. 'It was an accident. I never meant to turn innkeeper but I saw at once that it was an occupation that would suit me. My only talent is a knack for organisation.'

'From what I have heard the Peacock needed rather more than that,' he interjected.

'It was in a dreadful state,' she admitted. 'But the money Papa had given me was sufficient to cover the necessary repairs to the roof and for fitting everything else up in style.'

'*You* paid for the work to be done?'

'Naturally,' Athena said crisply. 'There is no

need to look so astonished, my lord. How else was I to persuade Tom Shaw into a partnership? It was a good bargain. I no longer need worry about providing a home for myself and Sherry and I have enough capital left over for my investments. Not that Papa would approve of my dabblings on the 'Change. He wanted me to use the money to pay for a trip to Ireland but I hate the place and I haven't seen my godmother since I was a baby so we quarrelled, of course.'

'I'm damned if I can make head or tail of this,' Nick declared frankly. 'You had better tell me the whole story. We can sit down over there out of the wind.'

Athena surveyed the grassy bank he indicated.

'Aren't you afraid it might be damp?' she enquired with a provocative glance at his elegant attire.

'My God, she thinks me a curst dandy!' Nick raised a pained hand to his brow and a gurgle of laughter escaped Athena.

'Oh, no, sir, a dandy would never deign to be seen carrying a straw basket filled with books!'

Fortunately, the grass was dry and once they had settled themselves Nick said, 'What's this about visiting your godmother? You have never mentioned it before.'

Athena shrugged. 'It was Papa's idea but he would not listen when I told him that nothing would induce me to live in the same neighbourhood as my grandfather—'

'The General, I assume?' Nick interrupted.

'I suppose Sir George told you I was related to him?' Athena asked, and when he nodded she continued in the same rapid voice. 'He is a detestable man. Papa was prepared to overlook his shabby behaviour but I am not! Two years ago we visited him in the hope of mending an old family quarrel but it was a waste of time. Far from agreeing to heal the rift, he told Papa that he no longer considered him his son!'

Athena snorted with indignation. 'I dare say Lady Fitzpatrick is all that is amiable but my grandfather is a near neighbour of hers and as her guest I would certainly meet him again. I doubt if I could be civil to him so it is better if I stay away. Imagine the scandal it would create if I snubbed him at one of her parties!'

'Aye, that would set tongues wagging!' Nick grinned for an instant at the picture she painted but then his tanned face sobered. 'Why did your father want you to go to Ireland? Surely you would have been better off living under his protection.'

A little sigh escaped Athena. 'Not in the circumstances,' she murmured.

'You needn't tell me more if it distresses you,' he said gently, sensing her hesitation.

Glancing up at him, Athena saw the concern in his dark eyes. Until this moment Sherry was

59

the only person she had ever confided in but her instincts told her that he would not be shocked.

'We have not known each other for very long but I feel that you are my friend and I do not wish to keep secrets from you,' she said slowly.

A few weeks ago Nick knew this candid declaration would have sent a surge of triumph pounding through his veins. He had achieved the conquest he had set out to win but it no longer mattered. All he was conscious of was the fact that she valued his friendship enough to trust him.

Burning with a desire to chase that look of worry from her face, he said eagerly, 'Perhaps I can provide a fresh insight.'

'My father is an inveterate gamester,' she began, strangely relieved to be able to talk about it at last. 'All my life I've known he couldn't be trusted not to gamble away our last shilling. Oh, there have been times when we lived magnificently! He is a very generous person, you see, but his luck has been poor ever since we returned to England. Finally, last January, his creditors were about to pounce so he decided to flee to the Continent. He wanted me to go with him. He had this wild idea that he could open a gaming house in Vienna, but I was tired of forever travelling.'

A hint of bitterness crept into her tone. 'We never had a settled home. I used to watch how the worry and strain of it all made my mother ill. She died when I was twelve and Papa began to send me away to school. I suppose I was an inconvenience to him.'

Nick let out a low whistle of surprise. 'Don't tell me he was a rake as well as a gamester?'

She nodded, her disapproval obvious. A slight uneasiness possessed Lord Verlaine. Had she taken his warning seriously or had she imagined he was merely joking when he had told her of his own wild reputation?

'To be fair, I believe Papa was a faithful enough husband, but he maintained a string of mistresses after Maman's death,' Athena continued, and Nick forced himself to concentrate. 'Naturally, he was discreet, and Sherry said it was indelicate of me to take any notice, but I must admit I did resent them.'

A frown creased her brow. 'I have no wish to be introduced to any of Papa's lightskirts but I still think it is silly to have to pretend that I don't know that they exist just because I am unmarried.'

'Society imposes some stupid rules,' agreed Lord Verlaine, tactfully curbing his amusement at her frankness.

'Not that Papa let his personal life affect his choice of school for me. He took great care to select the best available. Once I even attended an expensive Bath seminary!'

'The apogee of any young lady's education, to be sure.'

61

His dry comment brought a fleeting smile of appreciation to her lips but it vanished when she spoke again. 'Of course, when his luck was bad, I'd be fetched back to his current lodgings until the next time there was any money to spare.'

Nick thought it was a tribute to her intelligence that she had surmounted these difficulties but decided she would think he was bamming her if he told her so.

'Occasionally Papa hired a governess for me instead but Sherry was the only one who stayed for any length of time. Maman had employed her as my nurse when I was a baby and she always responded whenever Papa sent for her, even though he did not always pay her wages.'

Athena's mouth twisted in a wry grimace.

'He is a very charming man, you see. People usually end up doing what he wants. He thought I would agree to his Viennese scheme but I resisted his persuasion. He was furious with me!' Her voice trailed away.

'So he went abroad and left you to your fate,' Nick concluded for her and she nodded.

A strong desire to land the absent Mr Delaney a facer began to possess Lord Verlaine and he could not prevent himself from saying hotly, 'It was infamous of him to abandon you like that!'

'What else could he do? Debtors' prison beckoned! What's more, I am of age and he could hardly drag me on board ship by the hair.' Athena flung out her hands in a telling gesture. 'In fact, he delayed as long as he could in order to try and talk me into visiting my godmother if I would not go with him. It is hardly his fault that I did not wish to be beholden to her but at least he knew I would be safe with Sherry and he gave me most of the money he had salvaged, which he could ill spare.'

A lock of raven hair tossed by the breeze strayed across her cheek and Athena brushed it impatiently aside.

'Most people think I am eccentric. I suppose you also consider me a fool to reject my godmother's aid in favour of this kind of life,' she muttered, her fingers plucking nervously at her skirts.

'Not in the least!' Nick possessed himself of her restless hands and held them in a comforting grip.

Athena's strong affection for her wastrel of a father had touched Nick deeply. She hadn't blamed Delaney for the strange situation she found herself in but had made the best of it and come about by sheer hard work. Far from despising her, Nick's respect for her courage was increased by hearing her story. She presented a brave front to the world but now he knew that she was far more vulnerable than people supposed. Beneath her determination he sensed that she longed for security.

'Didn't we just agree that we are friends?' Nick gave her hands a slight squeeze. 'And friends do not criticise each other, my dear Miss Delaney.'

Unconsciously, Athena began to relax. Until he had spoken so warmly, she hadn't realised just how much she had been dreading seeing his expression freeze with scorn.

'Don't you have any other relatives you could turn to?' Nick asked, carefully releasing her after a moment.

Vaguely wishing he had not observed the proprieties, Athena shook her head. 'Papa was an only child and most of Maman's family perished during the Terror. I believe there may be some cousins still living in the Loire but Papa lost contact with them years ago.' She shrugged lightly. 'Not that it signifies. I would not trouble strangers for help.'

He was staring at her with a thoughtful frown on his handsome face.

'Come, sir, don't look so gloomy. I cannot think what possessed me to burden you with my tale of woe.' She gave a rather artificial laugh. 'Do forget my nonsense, I implore you.'

'You ought to get married,' he said abruptly, ignoring her attempt to change the subject.

A sudden flush of colour stained the skin over Athena's high cheek-bones.

'Now you sound like Sherry,' she replied, oddly breathless. 'She wants me to marry William Taylor.'

Nick stared hard at her, a muscle flickering at the corner of his well-cut mouth. 'Does she, by God?'

An imp of mischief prompted Athena to murmur, 'It would be a suitable match, I suppose.' She cast him an innocent glance. 'He is a very respected man hereabouts.'

'He is a pompous idiot!' Nick glared at her. The shaft of jealousy that tore through him was unbearable.

'William might be a little stiff-necked but you cannot accuse him of being stupid!'

Since Nick knew this protest to be justified he curbed a desire to curse, contenting himself by saying grimly, 'Marry him and you'd be bored to tears within a week of the wedding.'

'I *knew* you did not like him!' A peal of laughter escaped Athena but her merriment swiftly faded. 'Oh, dear, I should not have teased you when you have been so very kind to me this morning. Please don't look so cross.'

The tension in the pit of Lord Verlaine's stomach uncoiled. 'Then you aren't serious about marrying him?'

'I have no wish to marry anyone! In my experience, matrimony does not bring happiness. I have never met a couple who were truly content with one another.'

'My sister is happily married.' Nick was surprised to hear himself defending an institution he had hitherto despised.

'Then she is a lucky woman,' Athena

retorted. 'No doubt I am prejudiced, but it has always seemed to me that women lose their rights when they marry. They are expected to become mere shadows of their husbands, but I have grown to value my freedom while I have been in Parkgate. It is hard supporting oneself but at least I can make my own decisions. Marriage is too risky a business!'

Until a few weeks ago Lord Verlaine, a confirmed bachelor, would have had no hesitation in agreeing with this sensible statement. It was unsettling to realise that his sentiments were no longer so clear-cut.

'Then you don't believe in love?' he asked slowly.

'Love?' Athena's Celtic eyes blazed. 'If you ask me that is a fairy-tale invented by men to dupe their victims into doing exactly as they wish. Our happy acquiescence is assured because we imagine ourselves cherished and adored whereas in reality we are nothing more than playthings to be ignored at will.'

This spirited declaration made Lord Verlaine blink.

'You have a very poor opinion of my sex, ma'am,' was all he could manage to utter.

The fact that she had nonplussed a gentleman renowned for his polished address seemed to afford Miss Delaney no satisfaction. She merely shrugged and avoided his gaze.

Staring hard at the ground and pretending an urge to crunch the fallen leaves beneath the heel of her crimson jean half-boot, Athena wondered what on earth had possessed her to make such an outrageous statement. In her heart of hearts she knew it wasn't true. Even if she had once thought very little of most of the men she had encountered, she was now painfully aware that it was possible to find a man who was neither boring nor a rogue. The proof sat beside her.

'Are you by any chance a devotee of Mrs Mary Wollstonecraft?' Nick enquired, breaking the silence.

The realisation that her former beliefs had undergone a drastic change was so disturbing that Athena almost missed the point of this query.

'What? Oh, I see. Yes, I have read her book, *Vindication of the Rights of Women*, but I do not agree with all she says.'

'Thank God for that!'

His wry expression brought the smile back to Athena's lips. 'Nor, in case you are wondering, does my past contain an unhappy love-affair which has left me broken-hearted and embittered,' she added lightly.

This solution had occurred to Lord Verlaine, but he was happy to see it demolished.

'I cannot even lay claim to a schoolgirl infatuation. Not one of the countless dancing-masters and music-teachers I encountered made the least dent in my heart,' Athena continued in the same vein. 'No doubt my nature must be cold.'

Remembering her passionate response to his kiss, Nick raised his eyebrows in disbelief.

Possibly the same thought occurred to Miss Delaney, for she immediately hurried on, 'In any event, I think Sherry is mistaken. I do not think William Taylor would wish to marry me. He is just a friend.'

'There's more to it than that!'

Athena considered this remark. 'I dare say you are right. We share the same interest in financial affairs but it is my travels on the Continent that intrigue him. He has never had the opportunity to go farther afield than London and he likes to hear me speak of foreign places.'

Nick wondered if she was being wilfully blind. No doubt Taylor was flattered by her requests for advice and he was obviously impressed by her air of worldly sophistication but could she not see that the man was in love with her in his dry fashion?

It hadn't taken Nick above a few moments in the banker's company to realise this fact. That Athena herself was ignorant of the truth was astonishing and he could only conclude she had decided to regard Taylor as a friend and the notion was too firmly fixed in her mind to be shifted.

Pondering this revelation, Nick decided that his powers of perception regarding

Miss Delaney must be heightened. She had intrigued him from the day that they had met and that initial attraction had swiftly deepened.

She fascinated him! Half worldly sophisticate, half vulnerable innocent, she was like no other woman he had ever met. She was intelligent and outspoken, and her desire for independence was almost as unusual as her methods of obtaining it. She was capable of discussing matters normally considered a male preserve and yet she remained none the less a most deliciously feminine creature.

She was an enigma! Most puzzling of all was her avowal that she wanted none of love. It's like waving a red flag at a bull, Nick thought ruefully. How could any man resist such a delicious challenge!

And yet . . . she trusted him! How could he abuse her faith in him by making love to her unless he was sure he meant it? And for the first time in his life he wasn't sure about anything at all except a certainty that he didn't want to hurt her.

You are a fool, Verlaine, Nick thought to himself sardonically, but, high ideals not withstanding, the urge to draw her into his embrace and kiss her nonsensical ideas into the oblivion they deserved was so strong that he had to exert every ounce of will-power to resist it.

Instead, he grasped the basket lying beside

him and rose swiftly to his feet. 'We shall both be stiff with rheumatism if we sit here an instant longer,' he remarked easily as her surprised gaze flew to his face. 'That wind's turned curst cold.'

He stretched out his hand to assist Athena to her feet.

Taking it, Athena felt her safe, familiar world dissolve around her.

A moment ago he had held her hand to comfort her. His clasp had been steady. Now it trembled. She glanced up at him. He was pale beneath his tan and his eyes were glittering . . .

'Thank you,' she murmured, hardly daring to breathe.

She had made no move to withdraw. Her lovely face was still upturned to his, her eyes smiling in shy invitation, the tender curve of her pink mouth only inches away . . .

Nick released her hand quickly. 'Let's go and find this famous promenade of yours,' he said, fighting temptation.

Athena swallowed her disappointment. 'Of course.'

*   *   *

Athena placed the hip-bath in front of the fire in her tiny bedroom, for the November evening was chilly. Filling it from a succession of brass cans of hot water, she added a liberal dash of jasmine essence.

It was two weeks since she had confided in Nick on that grassy bank in Drury Lane and although she had seen him on several occasions since they had never been private together. Luxuriating in the warm scented water, Athena's thoughts returned yet again to that day.

He wanted to kiss me, I know he did! And I wanted him to, she admitted to herself honestly. Why had he drawn back? Athena suspected that her own sharp tongue was to blame. After the way she had ruthlessly criticised the whole male sex, he probably thought she detested all men!

But Nick is different, she thought. He made every other man she knew seem insignificant. She enjoyed his company and valued the friendship which had grown between them, but there was more to it than that.

I am in love with him, she thought wonderingly, acknowledging the truth at last. A great tide of joy surged through her entire being as she allowed herself to drop her defences and admit it. How could she have not realised it before? She wanted to be with him, to share his hopes, his fears, his whole life.

The only question was whether Nick felt the same. That he desired her she did not doubt. She had seen it in his eyes, but was that all he wanted from her? She didn't know. Desire is not the same thing as love, Athena told herself sternly, but she couldn't prevent her heartbeat from quickening as she completed her preparations for the ball.

Barton Grange was brilliantly lit as Athena and Sherry stepped down from the gig loaned to them for the evening by Tom.

'You will find refreshments in the kitchens, Jethro,' Athena informed him and he nodded happily.

Several damsels not blest with her looks sighed enviously as Athena appeared. Her ravishing gown of white tulle shrieked of Paris while her black curls were dressed *à la Sappho* and the glow in her eyes outshone the pretty little sapphire pendant that encircled her slim white neck.

'Damme if I've ever seen you in such looks!' her host exclaimed as she made her curtsy, and only the reproving frown of his cousin checked George's continuing flight of admiration. Recalling decorum, he introduced Athena to Mrs Emily Brockenhurst.

After a moment they passed on into the ballroom George's grandfather had built in the East Wing to please his wife. Athena searched eagerly for Lord Verlaine but there was no sign of him. Reluctantly she allowed her dance-card to be filled, carefully saving the dance before the supper-interval.

She was taking part in a cotillion when her partner, a local farmer who was one of her most devoted admirers, said gruffly, 'Do you know that fellow over there, Miss Delaney?

He is staring at you.'

Athena turned and saw Nick leaning against a column watching her with a slight smile on his handsome face.

'Damned—I mean, dashed rude to stare like that! Shall I call him to account?'

There was a note of uncertainty in her young swain's voice, as if he suspected the task might prove beyond him. Athena, dragging her attention from the splendid figure Lord Verlaine cut in his impeccable evening-clothes, politely pretended not to notice, saying only, 'Indeed, you must not, Mr Briscoe. That gentleman is a friend of mine.'

'Oh, well, in that case!' Relief brightened her partner's expression. There was something faintly dangerous-looking about the big, tall man with the black hair. Secretly wishing that his coat sat so superbly across his shoulders and that he had the knack of tying his neckcloth so elegantly, Mr Briscoe risked no further objection when Athena desired him to escort her to Lord Verlaine after the dance ended.

'Breaking all the local hearts, I see,' Nick remarked with an amused look after the departing Mr Briscoe's stiff back.

'He thinks my choice undeserving,' Athena said severely, to hide the giddy pleasure his nearness aroused in her.

'How can I help staring when you look so lovely?'

Athena blushed. This simple compliment pleased her far more than Sir George's effusions, which she strongly suspected to be inspired by the bottle.

'George is a trifle flown,' Nick remarked, confirming her theory when she mentioned that the baronet did not seem his usual self. 'The relief of everything turning out as planned, I expect.'

Athena chuckled. 'It does look striking.'

Sir George's fancy had led him to have the ballroom draped in swags of patriotic red, white and blue silk and decorated with masses of hothouse flowers all in the same hues.

The sets began to form for the next dance and out of the corner of his eye Nick saw Athena's partner approaching.

'No doubt I am too late but will you dance with me?' he said quickly.

Athena pretended to consult her card. 'You may have the waltz before supper.'

'I shall look forward to it,' Nick replied with a great deal of truth.

Athena was talking to William Taylor when the musicians Sir George had hired struck up for the waltz, but she broke off her conversation in mid-sentence as she watched Nick come towards them, her pulses quickening.

The sight of his lordship did not afford Mr Taylor the same gratification.

I wish you would reconsider, my dear. The

waltz is still frowned upon by older persons as improper—'

'Fiddlesticks!' Athena interrupted briskly. 'I have danced it in the best houses in Europe.'

'Not with Verlaine as your partner,' William continued heavily. 'His reputation is none so sweet. You cannot wish people to think you favour him. They will say you are fast.'

Athena's eyes flashed dangerously. 'Thank you for your concern, William, but I believe it misplaced on this occasion. My credit will surely survive one dance with his lordship.'

He sighed. 'If you are set on waltzing, won't you accept me as your partner instead?'

'But I have already taken part in a quadrille with you and two dances would occasion the kind of gossip you seem so anxious for me to avoid,' Athena retorted.

Since this was undeniable, William was at a loss.

' 'Servant, Taylor,' said Lord Verlaine, reaching them. He bowed elegantly to Athena. 'Miss Delaney. I believe this is my dance.'

There was a hint of amusement in Nick's greeting, for he had discerned the banker's annoyance and guessed its cause. 'Have I cut you out, sir? Never mind, better luck next time.'

For an instant it looked as if William would forget his inherent caution and give vent to his injured feelings, before he shook his head and said coldly, 'It pleases you to jest, my lord, but my friendship with Miss Delaney does not rest upon such trivialities.'

'Excuse us, the dance is starting,' Athena intervened, laying her gloved hand upon Lord Verlaine's arm.

Nick led her out on to the floor and Athena immediately forgot about William's absurd homily. Nick's arm clasped her lightly to him and she surrendered to bliss as he whirled her round in perfect time to the music.

Their steps matched as if they had danced together a thousand times. 'You dance divinely,' Nick murmured in her ear. 'You are as light as a fairy.'

Breathlessly, Athena laughed. 'What nonsense, sir!' She felt as if she had been drinking vast quantities of champagne instead of just one glass.

Looking up into his face, she saw that he was smiling at her with such an expression of warmth that her heart thundered against her ribs.

His arm tightened around her waist. 'You know what I would like to do now?'

'Dare I ask?' she murmured irrepressibly.

He grinned. 'Well, of course I would like to kiss you, but not here! No, I'd like to take you to see George's lake. There is a beautiful moon. Wouldn't you like to escape from this crowd, sweetheart?'

Athena was sorely tempted by this improper suggestion.

'I cannot think Sherry would approve,' she said with a little catch of longing in her voice.

'You think me incapable of turning her up sweet?' Nick enquired with a wicked chuckle.

'I'm sure you could!' Athena shook her head reprovingly at him. 'You must know you are a favourite with her in spite of your—' She broke off abruptly.

'In spite of my disgraceful reputation,' he finished for her, the smile vanishing from his face.

Athena coloured, wishing she had not allowed her tongue to run away with her.

Silence descended and while Athena was desperately casting around for some means of letting him know that there was nothing she would like better than to be alone with him in the moonlight Nick was thinking hard.

He was not accustomed to putting the needs of others before his own desires. Generously indulging any mistress to the top of her bent, he'd dismissed them the instant he tired of their company. It hadn't occurred to him until now that his behaviour had been self-centred but as he gazed down into Miss Delaney's flower-like countenance he knew that he didn't want to hazard any romp which would risk her reputation.

'Forgive me, I should not have suggested such a thing. It would do you no good to be seen with me in such improper circumstances.'

His rueful apology tore Athena's remaining

composure to shreds. 'Oh, don't, Nick! I don't care what people might say; I want to be with you!'

The moment this impetuous confession left her lips Athena blushed, realising how forward she must sound.

'That's the first time you've used my name,' Nick said, tactfully pretending he hadn't heard the rest of her speech.

'Ah, but you called me sweetheart,' Athena pointed out lightly, recovering her poise by sheer will-power.

'So I did,' Nick agreed and they both burst out laughing.

Across the room William Taylor watched them, his expression blank. He did not hear his name being spoken until it was repeated a second time.

'George.' He turned reluctantly to greet the speaker.

'Hope you are enjoying my little party.'

'Of course,' William said politely, but he couldn't prevent his gaze from returning to the couple leaving the floor.

'You've met Verlaine? One of my oldest friends. Known him even longer than I've known you.' Sir George grinned jovially at the banker.

William forced a smile. They had been neighbours for many years.

'They make a handsome couple, don't they?' George chuckled. 'If I didn't know better, I might think Nick in danger of marching to the altar before he was much older.'

William's attention was caught.

'My dear George, whatever can you mean?' he asked smoothly, scenting a mystery that might, with any luck, discredit his rival.

George coughed and looked sheepish. 'Don't think I ought to say,' he muttered.

William chuckled. 'Oh, come now, surely you can tell me!'

Foggily George considered this request and concluded that there was no harm in sharing their little joke with another man of the world.

Meanwhile, Nick had taken Athena in to supper. She was far too excited to eat but sat happily sipping the champagne he had procured for her.

She had eyes for no one else. It was as if they were wrapped around by an enchanted bubble which excluded the rest of the world.

'I suppose we had better return to the ballroom,' she sighed when the informal meal was over.

'Your next partner will be waiting,' Nick agreed.

'I know,' Athena nodded dolefully.

'In fact, your dance-card is crowded,' he added, trying to ignore the hammer of his pulse.

Casting him a mischievous glance, Athena impulsively tore the little card in two.

'There, now I am free!' she laughed.

'Then I suggest we find a quiet spot to enjoy our freedom before we are besieged by a host of your angry admirers.' Nick's tone was light, giving no hint of the fierce emotions raging in him. His desire to be alone with her was so strong that it robbed him of his good intentions and he forgot that he had resolved not to jeopardise her reputation.

Without knowing quite how he accomplished it so neatly, Athena found herself swiftly whisked through the crowd. A maze of corridors led them to a small parlour, dimly lit by a few candles and a banked-down fire in the hearth.

'It is probably too cold to view the lake now but I think we should be safe from interruption here,' Nick announced.

Athena's hand abruptly released his arm and, looking down at her, Nick saw that she had turned pale.

'What's the matter, sweetheart?'

The silence was intense and Athena thought he must hear the thudding of her heart.

'Perhaps we should not have . . . that is . . .' She hardly knew how to frame her sudden unease. Until they had reached this lonely room their escape had seemed a game but their solitude abruptly brought home to her the gross impropriety of her conduct.

Lord Verlaine raised his brows. 'I see. You have had second thoughts.'

Athena hung her head. What must he think of her?

'Don't worry, I shall return you to Sherry if that is what you wish. But I wasn't planning to seduce you on the hearthrug, you know,' he reassured her in a tight voice.

The frightened mist cleared from Athena's brain. 'Oh, Nick, I'm sorry for being so missish! I did not mean to imply that you would behave in an ungentlemanly way.'

Her frank admission wiped the frown from his face.

'It is my fault; I should not have encouraged you,' she continued dolefully.

'I'm all for such delightful encouragement,' he murmured with a little chuckle. 'Oh, sweetheart, if we are to indulge in confessions, then I must admit I hoped for this,' he went on, taking her in his arms.

Miss Delaney made no move to pull away.

'And this,' he added softly, bending his head to hers.

His lips were warm and gently persuasive, coaxing a response until Athena forgot her fears and kissed him back, her mouth parting beneath his as their embrace became more passionate.

Desire coursed through Athena's veins and her arms came up to lock themselves behind his neck, one slim hand burying itself in the thick hair that clustered on his nape. Eagerly, she obeyed the prompting of her dazzled senses and pressed herself against the lean length of him.

Nick stifled a groan. He wanted her very much but she wasn't one of his practised flirts. For all her abandoned surrender, he was aware of her innocence, and he wasn't so steeped in dissipation that he would take advantage of it.

'Sweetheart, we had better go.' Reluctantly he disengaged her clinging arms and stepped back.

Athena's gaze was cloudy with passion as she stared up at him in bewilderment. 'Go?' she echoed blankly.

'If we linger here any longer, I'm afraid you'll make a liar of me,' he said gruffly.

Comprehension dawned on Athena and she blushed, looking so adorably confused that he instantly exclaimed, 'Oh, my darling girl!' and drew her back into the circle of his arms.

When at last he lifted his dark head again Lord Verlaine said thickly, 'Now we really must return before they send out search-parties to look for you.'

Athena giggled at the wry expression he pulled. 'Let them,' she murmured happily, as she laid her head against his shoulder with a voluptuous sigh of content.

'Minx!' Nick brushed his lips against the dark cloud of her hair. 'If we are to avoid gossip, I had best give you a wide berth for the rest of this evening but may I call upon you in the morning? There is something I must tell you.'

Athena quickly tilted her face up to his. Suddenly she thought she knew what it was that he wanted to say and elation made her smile even more bewitching as she replied, 'Of course you may.'

*　　*　　*

The sound of breaking crockery assaulted Lord Verlaine's ears as he handed over his horse into Jethro's enthusiastic care a little before noon the next day. The noise was even louder when he stepped inside the Peacock and to add to his surprise he saw William Taylor descending the stairs.

The banker was looking a trifle pale but his expression became triumphant when he noticed Nick. 'Good morning, my lord.'

'What the devil is going on?' Impatiently Nick ignored this greeting.

'You must discover that for yourself, sir.'

It puzzled Nick why the banker should sound so smug, but he had no time to waste on the fellow and with a murmured farewell took the stairs several at a time.

As he had suspected, the noise was coming from Athena's private parlour. He rapped on the door smartly and walked in.

'Oh, it's you!' Miss Delaney ejaculated in accents of loathing. A vase was in her hand and to Nick's astonishment she hurled it at his head.

Thanks to his swift reactions the ornament did not strike him but smashed against the wall. Surveying the fragments Nick exclaimed, 'Good God, Athena, have you run mad?'

This demand did nothing to soothe Miss Delaney's outrage. Her bosom heaved beneath its covering of jonquil muslin as she spat at him, 'Get out, you . . . you snake!'

Understandably bewildered, Lord Verlaine stared at her. 'Did Taylor say something to upset you?'

'William?' Athena emitted an unladylike snort. 'I might have known you would try to pin the blame on William when all he did was tell me the truth.'

A sinking sensation assailed Nick's stomach.

'The truth?' he murmured weakly.

'Oh, stop pretending! George told William all about your odious wager.'

'Ah! Actually, I was going to tell you about it myself,' he began, but she flung out a warning hand to silence him.

'Don't! There is no point in spinning me any more of your lies. Oh, how could I have been such a fool?' Tears of humiliation sparkled in Athena's eyes. She had behaved like a wanton hussy and now she was paying for it.

'Sweetheart, I know it looks bad, but believe me it isn't quite how it seems.' Nick took a step towards her, holding out his hands, but she backed away, a look of disgust on her face.

'Is there nothing you will not stoop to?' she exclaimed bitterly, wondering how she could have really believed that he cared for her when all the while he had been skilfully playing on her emotions to satisfy his own vanity. 'How can you pretend that you give a straw for my feelings when thanks to you I am made an object of mockery for the whole town to laugh at?'

'If that is what Taylor told you then he is a damned liar!' Nick exclaimed heatedly. 'My wager with George was a private one. I don't know how Taylor managed to persuade George to speak of it but I can assure you that I have never done so.'

Athena took a deep breath, trying in vain to compose herself. Did he expect her to be grateful for this forbearance?

'Listen to me.' Nick grasped her hands, ignoring her squeak of outrage. 'I should never had agreed to that idiotic wager. It was only a jest—'

'A jest!' Athena interrupted, her eyes blazing with fresh fury. 'You may think it amusing—I do not!'

Nick winced, cursing his unfortunate choice of words. God, he was handling this badly! Desperately he tried again. 'I only agreed out of pique. You seemed so indifferent that I wanted to teach you a lesson but I swear to you that I had forgotten my original motives long before the first week of our acquaintance was out.'

Athena tugged her hands free. 'I don't believe you,' she said flatly.

Anger began to stir in his lordship.

'Good God, girl, if I had intended to seduce you do you think I would have missed last night's opportunity?'

The angry flush faded from Miss Delaney's cheeks and, seeing how she trembled, Nick regretted his blunt remark. 'Oh, damn!' he muttered. 'I should not have said that.'

Athena bit her lower lip. 'There are very many things you should not have said to me, my lord,' she declared unsteadily.

She could have forgiven him the wager. Men possessed such odious habits, as she knew only too well, but he had done more than exercise his charm. He had pretended to be her friend and, remembering how she had confided in him, she wanted to weep.

'I should have told you earlier but I knew you would be angry so I delayed.' Nick smiled at her ruefully. 'Now Taylor has beat me to it and I am well served for my cowardice but I give you my word of honour that I never meant to hurt you.'

Athena stared at him. He looked so earnest that for an instant she was almost tempted to believe him but then she shook her head. She had made the mistake of trusting him once already and it had brought her only heartbreak.

'Your word of honour is worthless. Men of your stamp will say anything to achieve their aims,' she stated coldly, concealing her despair. 'Your apology is as false as your friendship and I want none of it. Now please go; there is nothing more to be said.'

'There you are mistaken, you little termagant!'

Nick seized her by the shoulders and shook her roughly. 'By God, how dare you accuse me of trifling with you when I came here this morning intending to apologise? I was even going to ask you to marry me!'

Since it was this romantic expectation that had sent Miss Delaney off to bed on a cloud of blissful hope, her reaction was all the more fierce. 'Oh, how dare you make a mock of me?' she gasped, struggling to free herself.

Guessing her intention was to box his ears, Lord Verlaine kept a tight hold on her and ploughed on.

'Perhaps I should not have spoken just yet but I assure you my sentiments are sincere. I would consider it a great honour if you would accept my hand in marriage.'

It never occurred to Athena that he might be feeling so shaken that his customary address had deserted him, leaving him as self-conscious as a callow youth. She had never seen him lose mastery over himself and thought his exaggerated formality was just another mocking jest.

If she had been pale before, it was as nothing compared to the deathly pallor that now robbed her of every last vestige of colour. For an instant Nick was worried that she might swoon before she recovered her breath enough to speak.

'You must think me very green not to know that you are laughing at me—'

'Laughing at you!' exclaimed his lordship, thunderstruck. 'You little idiot, I love you!'

'How very obliging of you, but I fear I cannot return your affection, sir,' Athena retorted bitingly.

Her sarcasm made Nick flinch and release her as if he had been burnt. 'My God, you really believe that I asked you just to insult you,' he said slowly.

'I believe that you are a rake and the sort of man I despise,' Athena declared in a shaking voice. 'I doubt if you even know the meaning of the word love. It is merely that you are not used to being rebuffed and you are so piqued that you are willing to go to any lengths to avoid being bested.'

'If that is what you truly think then I see it is useless for me to seek to persuade you otherwise,' Nick said stiffly.

'Just go,' said Athena tragically, her last lingering hope that he would deny her accusations fading. Oh, why hadn't he sought harder to convince her of his feelings? Surely he would have at least tried to kiss her if he really loved her, instead of standing there like a statue?

'Gladly, ma'am.' Lord Verlaine executed a graceful bow, and, turning on his heel, left the room.

His departure, far from pleasing her, prompted Miss Delaney to burst into tears, the first she had shed since she was twelve years old.

CHAPTER FOUR

'My dear, won't you come and sit by the fire? These February evenings can be so treacherous and I do not want you to catch a chill after your long journey. There now, are you quite comfortable?' Lady Fitzpatrick beamed upon her guest and rattled on without giving Athena time to answer. 'I hope you found your room to your satisfaction. My daughter Cathleen helped me choose the curtains for it, you know. The ones we found hanging were so shabby, a fault, I'm afraid, of hired houses. Not that I expected such a thing in Cavendish Square, which I was told was a superior address.'

She paused for a moment to hand Athena a cup of tea.

'I have told them to take a tray up to Miss Sherrington. The poor woman looked quite done in! Unlike my son, who rushed off to Tattersall's the minute we arrived from Ireland!' She laughed merrily. 'You shall meet them both at dinner, my dear. Cathleen was wild with excitement when she heard you were coming to pay us a visit but unfortunately she was promised to Lady Hetherbridge this afternoon and could not stay to greet you.'

'I am looking forward to meeting your children, ma'am,' Athena murmured, feeling somewhat dazed by this flood of information.

Her godmother beamed upon her and immediately launched into an eulogy concerning her offspring, giving Athena time to take discreet stock of her surroundings.

The drawing-room in which they sat was elegant. Furnished in the latest style, the walls were hung in pale green silk, which served as an admirable foil for her hostess's auburn hair.

Lady Fitzpatrick's appearance was, in fact, much as Athena had imagined from her father's description. She was a dashing widow in her early forties; her figure had lost its youthful slenderness but her face still retained charm. What did surprise Athena was her propensity to worldly chatter. Listening to the rambling monologue, she decided that her godmother was kind but rather shallow.

'To think that the last time I saw you was at your christening, my dear. You have grown into a beauty like your mama.' Lady Fitzpatrick sighed sentimentally. 'I was so pleased when Miss Sherrington wrote to me.'

Athena bit her lip, wondering how to answer her.

Prompted by the grey despair which had engulfed her young friend since Lord Verlaine's departure for his hunting-box near Grantham, Sherry had eventually written to Lady Fitzpatrick without Athena's knowledge. When the answering letter had come at the end of January bearing an invitation to visit her godmother, now residing in Cavendish Square, Athena had been angry and refused to go.

'Why not, might I ask?' Sherry had demanded. 'There is nothing to keep us here and a change of scene could only benefit your spirits.'

Knowing that she had been poor company in spite of all her efforts to hide her misery, Athena took refuge in saying that Tom needed them, but Sherry quickly dismissed this excuse.

'Now that the festive season is over Tom can manage very well on his own. Your godmother has written a very pretty letter, pointing out it is time you renewed your acquaintance with her, and since she is over here to give her family a taste of London life it will be no trouble to include you in her plans. Now, are you going to take advantage of her offer, which as you very well know was what your papa intended for you, or are you going to sit here nursing a broken heart forever?' she had added craftily.

This spurred Athena to action as she had hoped it might and before she could change her mind Sherry had booked places for them on the stage from Chester. To travel post was a luxury they could not afford and any objections Athena might have had were swiftly dispelled by William Taylor's protests when he arrived on his customary weekly visit.

'My dear Athena, you cannot travel on the common stage!' he stated, wagging one finger at her as if she were a wayward child. 'If you must go to London, and I own it sounds an excellent scheme, though I shall miss you sorely, then let me arrange a post-chaise for you.'

She stared at him and shook her head. 'I cannot allow you to frank me, William.'

'It would give me the greatest pleasure, but it won't be necessary.' He smiled at her. 'You see, I have something very important to tell you.'

Unease stirrred in Athena. For almost a year she had persisted in thinking him merely a friend but lately it had been borne in on her that she was mistaken. Sherry had always prophesied he would make her an offer and even Nick had insisted that William was in love with her.

She bit her lip at the memory, unable to bear thinking about his lordship. His perfidy had wrecked their golden autumn idyll but she missed him more than she had dreamt it was possible to miss anyone, and his absence had reduced her existence to a grey wasteland.

Slowly she became aware that William was still speaking.

'I beg your pardon; what did you say about the Vale of Clywd mine?'

William laughed heartily. 'Ah, my dear, I'm not surprised that you are wool-gathering at the thought of such riches coming your way.'

Urgently she requested him to repeat his explanation and then to his astonishment she burst out laughing.

'An income of eight thousand a year, you say? That makes me an heiress!' she choked, her mirth becoming slightly hysterical.

'My dear, shall I procure you a glass of hartshorn and water?' William asked uneasily, wishing that Miss Sherrington was not out marketing.

Athena coughed and forced down her unseemly amusement. 'I'm sorry, William. It was a shock, you see.'

'Well, it is rare that I can give a client such excellent news,' he conceded with as much satisfaction as if he had suggested the investment in Davis's mine, rather than opposed it. 'Now all that remains for us to do is decide how to re-invest this windfall. Of course there is no need for you to economise on travelling to London and no doubt you will wish to buy a few new gowns when you are there, but you must put the rest of the money to work. I'm sure you will be guided by my advice this time for such a wonderful stroke of luck is not likely to befall you again.'

His complacency caused Athena to lift her brows a little. Rather angrily she remembered that it was his interference that had provoked the disastrous quarrel with Nick. William intended nothing but good but his attitude rankled.

'You must not make it a habit to try and run my life for me, William,' she said coolly.

'Ah, but I hope that you will give me permission to do so in the near future, my dear.'

To Athena's dismay he then proceeded to go down on one knee and launch into an elaborate marriage proposal.

'Pray do get up,' she begged him. 'I am very obliged to you, but really we should not suit.'

William threw her an indignant look, since he hadn't finished. His feelings were further lacerated when she continued to refuse his gracious offer. It had never occurred to him that she might do so and he was deeply offended.

'I declare, Athena, if you think this money will bring suitors flocking then you are a fool,' he said heatedly. 'Your odd behaviour in Parkgate must offend any gentleman of quality.'

'Really?' Athena's feeling of guilt vanished.

'Then I wonder why you bothered to ask me to marry you, William.' She gave him a long cool look. 'I assume it is because my company has become a habit with you, since I do not wish to insult you by supposing it is my windfall that made me suddenly acceptable.'

He had the grace to colour, for, in fact, it was the success of her investment that had tipped the scales. He was very fond of her but it was not part of his plans to marry a penniless girl.

'My affection is genuine,' he began to protest, but Athena flung up her hand to cut him off.

'I do not doubt you think so, but it would not survive the rigours of marriage, sir. My taste for independence would drive you wild!' She did not add that he would soon bore her to distraction, but smiled at him sympathetically. 'Come, please do not spoil our friendship. Let us at least part on a civilised note and then perhaps when next we meet we can pretend this never happened.'

Reluctantly he had accepted this olive-branch, but, remembering that awkward scene as she listened to her godmother outlining the list of sights she intended to show her, Athena restrained a sigh.

She had come to London to please Sherry and because she couldn't think of anything else to do in spite of acquiring all that money. William's proposal had brought home how silly she had been to think that happiness depended on being secure from poverty. She had achieved the fortune she had set out to win but she had never been more miserable in her life!

No, happiness couldn't be found in material things. It didn't even depend on marrying a safe, solid man as she had once imagined it might. William was both those things but she had turned down the settled home he offered.

I don't want security, she admitted to herself sadly, I want Nick! It doesn't matter that he is a rake; he is the only man for me because I love him and that's more important than anything else!

'My dear, is there something wrong?' Her god-daughter's continuing silence at last penetrated Lady Fitzpatrick's self-absorption.

'Only that I am more of my father's daughter than I thought,' Athena murmured ruefully, coming to the depressing conclusion that she should have been more careful in what she wished for. A kind fairy had granted her longing for security but it had proved to be Dead Sea fruit! The only eligible husband for her was a rake, but, unfortunately, she had learnt this lesson too late!

*   *   *

Athena and Cathleen were sitting looking at the latest fashion magazines a few days before

Easter when Connor Fitzpatrick came bounding into the morning-room, a wide grin on his freckled face.

'I say, Athena, what's this I hear about you setting up as a London innkeeper? Mama's as mad as fire!'

'Do try for a little more conduct, Connor!' his sister scolded, making a hasty dive to rescue her property as he plumped down on to the sofa next to her. 'You know you should not ask embarrassing questions.'

Athena hid a smile. Connor reminded her of an overgrown puppy, sweet-natured but decidedly clumsy.

'Don't worry, Cathleen, I'm not offended,' she said. 'Nor am I ashamed of my plans. I intend to buy a small tavern called the White Bear in Bloomsbury. It is quite respectable and I have hopes of turning it into a hotel for visitors to London who cannot afford more fashionable hostelries. In fact, the agent handling the sale assures me that my idea is just what the area needs.'

Two identical pairs of hazel eyes stared at her in amazement before Cathleen exclaimed, 'But Athena, no one will ever receive you again if you dare do such a thing!'

Athena laughed. 'So your mama told me! She was nearly as vehement on the subject as Sherry, but really I don't care a fig.'

Connor let out a whistle of approval. He wished he dared scorn Society's opinion but there was still another year of his minority to go and his mother controlled the purse-strings. 'Well, I think it is a bang-up scheme,' he announced. 'Much more fun than hanging around drawing-rooms doing the pretty to a parcel of old dowagers!'

'Oh, how can you say so?' Cathleen rounded on him with a reproachful frown.

Just turned eighteen, she was enjoying her first taste of fashionable life and could not understand why anyone failed to find the whirl of parties, concerts, balls, plays and other similar amusements utterly enthralling.

Athena smiled at her. She was a pretty damsel, petite and slightly plump with her mother's auburn hair and pale skin, thankfully free of the freckles that afflicted her brother.

'You forget that such entertainments are not new to me, Cathleen. To please your mama and Sherry I have attended every function they suggested this last month or so but I have no taste to continue. Easter is upon us and it is high time I set up my own establishment.'

Recently, while the other ladies in the household rested to recruit their energies for the evening entertainments ahead, Athena had spent several afternoons being shown around likely inns by eager property-agents. The task had been more daunting than she was prepared to admit but she was determined to stick to her plans.

Spring had arrived and the blooming new

growth all around her was a poignant reminder that life was slipping pointlessly by. Perhaps if she could keep busy to the point of exhaustion—and surely running a hotel would tax all her energies—she would not have time to feel so unhappy. In all the hustle and bustle she might be able to forget the man she loved and if she could not then at least it ought to help ease her ever present sense of desolation.

The idea of returning to Parkgate was one she could not bear to contemplate. Every inch was imbued with memories of Nick and she knew that it would be hopeless to think she could escape her unhappiness there. London offered her the best chance of making a fresh start on her own terms. It was going to be very expensive but the money from Gareth Davis's copper mine would enable her to ignore what the *ton* might say.

Money was the subject also exercising young Mr Fitzpatrick's mind as he listened to his sister pelting Athena with questions about the White Bear. Uneasily, he thought of the multitude of unpaid bills secreted in the top drawer of his dressing-table. He had been convinced of his luck on the turf but his losses had been heavy and when added to the sums he had spent playing billiards at the Royal Saloon or drinking at the Daffy Club the amount was worrying.

Every penny of the generous allowance his mother had made him on their arrival in

London had been spent. But, fortunately, only that very morning a friend of his, Mr Barnabas Crutchley, had given him the name and direction of one of the more honest money-lenders. The slip of paper was in his pocket and he fingered it gratefully while forcing himself to pay attention to the conversation.

'Your grand announcement has thrown my little snippet of news into the shade,' Cathleen was saying plaintively.

She dimpled happily as Athena obligingly asked her what she meant. 'Well, you see, I met an acquaintance of yours last night at the opera. He asked after you most particularly! Mama said it was a pity that you had not elected to come with us for it seems he is a very eligible gentleman. And a very handsome one too!'

A languishing sigh accompanied this last remark and the blood ran cold down Athena's spine. 'His name?' she snapped in a tone that caused Cathleen's eyes to open very wide.

'Lord . . . Lord Verlaine,' she stammered.

The beat of her pulse thundered in Athena's ears. Her throat was suddenly too dry for her to speak and she was grateful when Connor broke the silence.

'Verlaine?' He cocked his red head on one side in thought. 'Tall, big-shouldered fellow with black hair?'

Cathleen affirmed it.

'Saw him t'other day at Jackson's. You

know, the boxing school in Bond Street.' Connor tried to look suitably casual, although he had been honoured by a word of praise from the great man himself after his bout with one of the ex-champion's assistants. 'Barney told me his name. Appears he's been in Devon, just inherited a fortune there. Some great-uncle stuck his spoon in the wall and left him everything. Lucky devil!' Connor sighed enviously.

Athena struggled to retain her composure. Nick had never mentioned a word of this possibility to her. In fact, now she came to think of it, he had never spoken of his own financial circumstances. She had assumed he lived on the edge of insolvency like so many retired army officers with expensive tastes and tactfully avoided any questions that might have embarrassed him.

'Mama has invited him to dine with us on Saturday evening,' Cathleen announced.

Athena leapt to her feet. 'Excuse me, I have something I must do.'

Connor and Cathleen stared in amazement as she rushed from the room. They would have been equally surprised if they could have overheard her conversation an hour later with the property-agent to whom she had fled.

'This is absurd, sir. I come here willing to meet your client's price and now you tell me that a new buyer is bidding against me.'

Mr Brown met her angry gaze

apologetically. 'I'm sorry, Miss Delaney, but business is business and Lord Verlaine has offered a higher—'

'Verlaine! Did you say Verlaine?' Athena exploded.

She left the agent's office in a rage. Too angry to return to Cavendish Square, she tried to walk off the worst of her fury in the Green Park, but all she could think of was Nick's despicable treachery.

He must have heard of her scheme from Lady Fitzpatrick, who was an incurable rattle. No doubt he had pretended concern, as an old friend of Athena's, and she had poured out her woes into his willing ears. Not that it really mattered how he found out; it was his spiteful interference that was so devastating.

He must be doing it for revenge! I wounded his pride and now he is extracting payment, Athena thought miserably. He must really hate me.

The idea hurt so much that she could hardly bear it but pride came to her rescue. The devil if she would sit tamely by and let him worst her! She was going to buy the White Bear if it killed her!

Where am I going to raise the extra money to outbid him at such short notice? she pondered, turning her footsteps for home.

This question was still vexing her when she descended to dining-room and it robbed her of any appetite for her luncheon. Luckily, Lady

Fitzpatrick did not notice in her concern for Connor, who also picked uninterestedly at his food, contrary to his usual custom.

'I'm all right, Mama,' he answered, brushing aside her enquiries.

They were leaving the table when he asked Athena in a whisper if he might have a word. Correctly interpreting that he wished the assignation to be kept secret, she nodded silently and went upstairs to wait for him in her room. A few moments later he tapped quietly on the door.

'Hate to bother you like this, Athena, but I don't suppose you could see your way to lending me a little blunt, could you?'

The notion of borrowing off his mama's rich guest had suddenly struck him during luncheon, but, meeting Athena's astonished gaze, Connor blushed.

'Sorry. Stupid idea,' he muttered, preparing to sidle out of the room.

'Wait! Are you in debt, Connor?'

'Can't discuss it with a lady,' he protested, but Athena responded with such sympathy that he found himself telling her all about it.

'Don't look so worried. You aren't the first young man to have gone wild when set loose on the town and I dare say you won't be the last.'

'No,' Connor replied heavily. 'But if you can't lend me the ready then it'll have to be the Jews for I cannot face Mama.'

'You mean a money-lender?'

He pulled out the scrap of paper from his pocket and handed it to her.

Athena's delicate brows rose.

'I think I had better keep this,' she murmured, trying to quell the sudden thudding of her heart. 'You won't need it. I shall settle your debts for you if you will but be patient.'

Connor's expressions of gratitude were prolonged but at last Athena managed to get rid of him.

She stared at the paper in her hand. Here was the solution to her dilemma if only she had the courage to take it. Papa had always decried the cent-per-cent bloodsuckers but her case was different. She *did* have money but not immediately to hand!

The image of Nick's darkly handsome face rose to taunt her and Athena's lovely mouth thinned. Jew Mendoza it was. She would not be beaten!

*　　　*　　　*

Athena dressed for dinner on Saturday evening as if for war. Her skilfully arranged locks, the clinging sapphire silk dress, her alluring perfume were her armour. Nick Verlaine was the man competing against her and she was determined to show no weakness.

The first sight of his tall figure clad in his

dark evening-clothes melted her resolve. Involuntarily, she moved towards him, her lovely smile lighting up her face. 'Nick!'

'Miss Delaney.' His voice was as cool as his bow.

Athena felt as if he had slapped her and her dismay increased when he turned to greet Cathleen with one of his engaging smiles.

Her godmother had arranged the table so that they were seated next to one another but Nick took no advantage of this privilege. Without being openly discourteous, he made it clear that he had no interest in her.

Despair destroyed what little remained of Athena's appetite. She toyed with her food, praying that the evening would come to an end.

Lady Fitzpatrick had arranged a visit to the Argyll Rooms to entertain her guests, but when the time came to leave Athena cried off, pleading a headache.

I cannot endure another minute of this torture, she thought, while assuring her godmother that she would be perfectly well again if she had a good night's sleep.

Athena was horribly conscious of Nick's eyes watching her. Did he know she was shamming it? Perhaps, but it hardly seemed to matter. Her last hope that their quarrel might be mended if only they could meet once more had been destroyed this evening.

'He doesn't love me any longer,' she

whispered to herself as she made her way to her room.

The words echoed in her head as the maid she shared with Cathleen helped her undress and get ready for bed. She couldn't seem to think of anything else. It was as if she was moving in a fog of numbness. Nothing seemed quite real.

'Goodnight, miss.'

The maid left the room and Athena picked up the book that lay on her bedside table, knowing that she could not settle to sleep. As she opened it a piece of paper fluttered out.

It was the address Connor had given her, which she had placed there for safety. Staring at it, Athena remembered her vow, and a spark of anger pierced her despair. Deliberately, she let it rekindle into flame, welcoming the rush of fury which blotted out the pain of Nick's rejection.

Athena flung back her bedclothes. Selecting a plain round gown, she began to get dressed again, her expression grim.

So, his lordship thought he could wreck her plans and then just dismiss her, did he? Well, she would teach him that he was wrong!

*   *   *

'What do you mean, man? Where can she have gone at this hour? It is nearly eleven.'

The young footman stared nervously at

Lord Verlaine.

'I can't rightly say, sir,' he mumbled. 'Miss Delaney just asked me to call a hackney and said I was to give this note to milady if they returned before she got back.'

'Give me that note,' Nick demanded.

'Sir! It's addressed to Lady Fitzpatrick,' the footman protested unhappily.

'Damn you for a fool, do you think her ladyship will object?' Nick growled, holding on to his temper by sheer effort. 'I shall take any blame but I must know where Miss Delaney has gone if I am to go after her. God knows what harm she might come to!'

Since the footman privately agreed it was shocking for a young lady, especially such a pretty young lady, to disappear into the night, he decided to obey his lordship's imperious request.

Scanning the single sheet, Nick let out a groan of incredulity. An alley off Tavistock Street! He restrained the impulse to tear at his black locks and confined himself to a few terse instructions.

He left the footman still nodding as he strode out to where his tilbury was waiting.

'I shan't need you any further tonight, Beech,' he told his groom.

Giving the spanking grey between the shafts the office to start, Nick drove off. He maintained a fast pace even when he reached Convent Garden, which was as usual crowded with strollers of all descriptions. Beyond the piazza, his surroundings became less salubrious, and his anxious frown deepened.

If Lord Verlaine could have but known it, Athena shared the same apprehension as her hackney threaded its way through the narrow, twisty streets. The entire area seemed composed of decaying hovels interspersed with mean little taverns. The darkness was lit here and there by flares and the light coming from the buildings, and she could see that the inhabitants were mostly ill-clad.

'I should not have come,' she whispered in dismay as the hackney turned into a narrow alley.

It drew to a halt before the only prosperous-looking house.

'Here we are, miss.' Disapproval was evident in the jarvey's voice.

Athena remained seated, her fingers nervously pleating her skirts. Dared she go in there alone? If she had known that the money-lender lived in such squalid surroundings she would have waited until she could have persuaded Connor to escort her.

'Are you getting out or what, miss? I can't wait here all night.'

His impatience acted as a spur, curing Athena's hesitation. 'Perhaps not, but you can at least wait until I have concluded my business,' she retorted briskly, jumping down. She flipped him a coin. 'Here, take this on account and don't worry—I shall pay you handsomely for your trouble.'

He grunted, but Athena ignored him and rapped smartly upon the door. After a long interval it was opened a crack by an old dame dressed in black.

'I wish to see Mr Mendoza,' Athena said with a calmness she was far from feeling. 'Here is my card.'

The sharp eyes surveyed her, taking in her plain but obviously expensive apparel. 'Come in.' Grudgingly the woman opened the door a further few inches, allowing Athena to pass inside.

'You should not have come on a Saturday. It is our holy day, and he don't like to do business 'cepting for special clients,' the old woman grumbled.

Athena slipped a coin into her hand. 'Please!'

'Wait here. I'll go and ask if he will see you.'

The hallway was bare and chilly and Athena's nervousness increased. She had the sensation that she was being watched, although she could see no one, and the minutes stretched out endlessly before the servant returned.

'He says you must come back tomorrow,' she announced.

'But tomorrow is Easter Sunday!' Athena exclaimed.

'Ain't of no interest to us.'

'No, I suppose not,' Athena laughed reluctantly. She had forgotten for a moment with whom she was dealing.

The old woman moved to open the door and Athena's flicker of amusement vanished.

'Wait! My business is urgent. I must see Mr Mendoza tonight.'

'Tomorrow,' said the custodian inexorably.

'But I shall not be able to get away!'

'Suit yourself.' She shrugged indifferently and began to bundle Athena out of the door.

It slammed shut in Athena's face, leaving her gasping with indignation.

Her indignation turned to dismay when she realised that her hackney had disappeared. She looked quickly up and down the length of the street but there was no sign of it.

Gritting her teeth, she began to walk rapidly, hoping that she could remember the way out of this maze of back streets. Hopefully she would be able to find another vehicle once she got nearer to Convent Garden.

She hadn't gone a hundred yards when she realised that she was being followed. Her heart began to pound and she quickened her steps.

'Hey, not so fast, little lady. Me and Tom here would like to talk to you.'

Athena swallowed hard. There were two of them, both scrawny and dressed in dirty rags with mufflers round their necks. She thought that they were probably rather younger than she was herself, but they looked tough, particularly the speaker, a blue-jowled individual with greasy hair.

'Get out of my way,' she snapped.

'Hoity-toity, ain't she, Tom?' An unpleasant smile twisted his mouth. 'C'mon, hand over your purse.'

'No!' Furiously, Athena knocked aside his searching hand. 'Leave me alone, you little rat.'

'You'll be sorry for that,' her assailant muttered, trying to grab her.

Athena screamed at the top of her lungs. At the same time she kicked him hard in the shins.

Her determined resistance startled them and for an instant they hung back.

Athena seized the chance and took to her heels.

'After her!'

Knowing she could not lose them on their home ground, Athena did not try to dodge and hide in one of the alleyways but ran straight on. She cast a glance over her shoulder. They were gaining on her. Hampered by her skirts, she couldn't outrun them.

A sob of fright escaped her as her foot slipped on a piece of decaying cabbage. Her balance lost, she tumbled to her knees.

'Got you!'

There was a hissing sound and the bully's cry of triumph was abruptly cut off.

Gasping for breath, Athena watched him lift

111

a dazed hand to his cheek and bring it away covered in blood.

The horsewhip sang swiftly through the air again, a deadly black snake in the hand of the tall man surveying them through narrowed eyes. It landed with a malevolent hiss, slicing open the second thief's bare arm. He gave a yell of pain and jumped backwards.

'C'mon!' He grabbed his friend, who was still standing in a stunned daze, and they turned tail.

The sound of their running feet faded and Athena looked up. So deep was her terror that she hadn't even heard the carriage draw up but now she recognised her rescuer as he leapt down to haul her ungently to her feet.

'Nick!'

He ignored her whisper of amazement and threw her up into the tilbury. 'That pretty pair might have friends,' he said tersely as he sprang up after her and set the grey in motion.

Soon the dingy streets were left behind and, her fear receding, Athena became aware of what a sight she must look. She had lost her bonnet and her pelisse was streaked with filth. Her hands shook as she lifted them to tidy her disordered hair and she saw that they were dirty too.

'This isn't the way back to Cavendish Square. Where are you taking me?' she asked a moment later, breaking the silence.

'To my sister's.' He glanced at her and

smiled suddenly. 'Don't look so worried. Verena is never shocked.'

Athena's spirits soared. At last he was the man she had known in Parkgate and not some distant stranger.

Mrs Gresham lived in a pretty little house in Stratton Street. To Nick's relief all the lights were shining when they arrived.

He handed Athena the reins. 'Let me have a quick word with her before I take you in,' he said.

The grey was too well schooled to require Athena's attention and her imagination ran riot during the few moments Nick was absent but she tried to appear calm as she allowed him to hand her down.

'My poor dear!' Verena Gresham's sympathetic smile enfolded her. 'Would you like to come with me and wash your hands while they make you some tea? I have ordered it to be served in the front parlour. Nick can wait for you there.'

Athena nodded shyly. She followed her hostess, who was amazingly like her brother with the same dark hair and eyes, up the narrow staircase to what was obviously a spare bedroom.

Mrs Gresham intercepted the ewer of hot water at the door and Athena was grateful for her tact.

'There is not much we can do about your pelisse, I'm afraid, but at least your dress is

113

only stained about the hem,' she remarked as Athena removed the offending mantle. 'Now, would you like me to help you with your hair?'

Athena accepted gratefully. Her hands were still unsteady.

Verena Gresham's dark eyes brimmed with curiosity, but, mindful of her brother's request, she restrained the questions that were burning her tongue as she rearranged Athena's curls into a semblance of order.

'There, I think you'll do,' she said in an encouraging tone. 'We had better go down before Nick frets himself to flinders.'

At the door to the parlour Mrs Gresham halted. 'I won't come in with you. I'm sure you will wish to discuss matters with my brother in private.'

Feeling rather like a Christian martyr about to be thrown to the lions, Athena walked into the parlour.

Nick was standing staring into the fire but he turned swiftly at her entrance. A few quick strides and he had crossed the room to her side.

'You little fool!' he said thickly, taking her into his arms.

Athena clung to him. 'Oh, Nick! Nick!'

Her lips parted as his mouth caressed hers with searing passion. Their breath mingled and as their tongues touched Athena felt a flame of pleasure igniting that strange liquid heat in the pit of her stomach. It was the same dizzying flood of desire that had swept over her the very first time he had taken her in his arms and she knew she never wanted to let him go.

'I like it when you kiss me,' she whispered huskily when at last he lifted his dark head.

'Good, because I intend to do so frequently, you adorable minx!' Nick replied, his dark eyes lighting with tender laughter.

She blushed and he tightened his arms around her.

'Oh, sweetheart, what a fright you gave me! What on earth possessed you to go to such a disreputable place?'

His question restored Athena to sanity. She pulled away from him. 'How did you know where I had gone?' she countered warily.

Nick shrugged. 'I ordered Lady Fitzpatrick's footman to hand over your letter.'

Athena gasped but before she could say a word he calmly swung her up into his arms and carried her over to the sofa by the fire, where he sat down, keeping her firmly on his knee.

'Now listen to me, you beautiful goose, I had to follow you. How else was I to apologise?'

Deciding it would be undignified to struggle, Athena sat still but she eyed him dubiously. 'Apologise?'

'For my ridiculous behaviour during dinner.' Nick shook his head and sighed. 'You'll never know how difficult it was to ignore you but I was determined to show you that I no longer cared. The moment I saw you again I knew it was no use but my curst pride wouldn't allow me to admit it.'

He fell silent, remembering how his conscience had smote him at the sight of her little wan face as she had made her excuses to the company before saying goodnight. She had tried so hard to appear composed but her eyes had betrayed her.

Their stricken expression had haunted him, making him cut short his entertainment and return to Cavendish Square, intending to have it out with her for once and all. But she had vanished and the circumstances in which he had next found her had driven every thought of recrimination out of his head. She could have been seriously hurt, killed!

The shock had brought home to him just how much he needed her. Their disastrous quarrel no longer mattered. Nothing mattered except the fact that he loved her.

Nick swallowed hard, trying to summon the courage to risk putting his fate to the touch. Did her wonderfully responsive kiss mean what he hoped or would she spurn him once more?

Before he could decide Athena said softly, 'I thought you might be going to apologise for trying to stop me buying the White Bear.'

It was very strange but somehow it no longer seemed important—still, she was curious. 'Was it revenge, Nick?'

'Of course not!' His indignant glare faded. 'I was trying to stop you making a social outcast of yourself. It seemed to me that you would be unhappy once the novelty had worn off but by then it would be too late.'

'Why should you care if I ruined my life?' Athena whispered, unable to meet his gaze.

'Because I love you,' he said simply. 'I told you once before and you would not believe me, but it is true. I have tried to forget you but I can't.'

How could he explain that she had given his life new meaning? When he was with her his restlessness dissolved and he was happier than he had been in years.

His arms tightened around her waist. 'You are a fever in my blood and I shall never be cured, my darling, unless you marry me.'

Athena threw her arms around his neck and hugged him fiercely. Her throat felt suddenly tight and for an instant she thought she might cry. 'Oh, Nick, you don't know how I have longed to hear you say you still cared,' she murmured.

She gazed wonderingly into his eyes and saw her own love reflected there.

'My beautiful girl.' Nick traced his forefinger gently down her cheek to touch her mouth with a butterfly lightness but when he would have kissed her Athena drew back.

'First, you deserve to know the truth,' she

said, steeling herself. 'I went to that dreadful place intending to borrow money so that I could outbid your offer.'

'Did I make you that angry?'

To her relief he was gazing at her with a rueful smile.

'You aren't disgusted by my behaviour?'

'Sweetheart, if I wanted some conventional little ninny ready to agree with my every word, then I should settle for someone like your pretty Cathleen.'

For an instant, jealousy darkened Athena's sapphire eyes but it faded as he continued. 'But I don't. I want you. You, my love, with your funny notions of independence and outrageous ideas. Just you, that's all I need to make me happy.'

'I don't think I do want to be independent any more,' Athena admitted candidly, her hand sliding of its own volition to twine itself into his hair. 'Not if it is at the cost of love. I've learnt that lesson at least.'

Nick grinned. He wondered how long this mood of humility would last. Not that he cared. Marriage with Athena might bring its own problems, but it would never be boring!

'You haven't answered my other question, you know,' he reminded her. 'Will you marry me, my dear Miss Delaney?'

'I should be honoured, my lord,' she replied gravely, but her eyes sparkled with laughter.

'I adore you!'

His lips took passionate possession of hers and Athena's laughter died. Her heart raced and she felt a surge of overwhelming desire tingling in every nerve. Pressing herself even closer to him, she kissed him back with a wanton fervour that left them both breathless.

'I didn't know it was possible to feel so happy,' she murmured when the long intoxicating kiss was over.

He smiled at her but before he could speak the ormolu clock on Mrs Gresham's marble mantelpiece chimed the hour.

Athena started up in alarm. 'Nick, look at the time! What will they be thinking in Cavendish Square?'

Lord Verlaine pulled her firmly back down on to his lap.

'If they have returned, which I beg leave to doubt, I hope your godmother's footman will have the sense to relay the message I left for her.'

'She might not feel so anxious if she knows I am with you,' Athena admitted.

'Your godmother is a woman of the world. I mentioned that I hoped to start a new life on my country estate and she thinks you will make me an admirable chatelaine.'

This remark made Athena survey him narrowly. 'Why did you not tell me that you were a rich man?'

'I wasn't until my uncle died,' he answered mildly.

'But you had sufficient for your needs?' she persisted.

'It seemed tactless to mention it.'

'So I let my prejudice trick me into thinking you must be penniless,' she said ruefully, and then suddenly realised something else. 'You told my aunt that you wanted to marry me?'

'I did hint at it,' he confessed. 'It seemed a good way to enlist her aid.' He grinned at her. 'She's right, you know, sweetheart. I can't imagine any one more suited to restoring old Uncle Nathan's property to order.'

'I see. You are marrying me for my housekeeping skills,' Athena retorted.

He shook his head. 'Actually, I had your other talents in mind.'

She eyed him quizzically. 'Such as?'

'This . . . and this, my love,' he whispered tenderly, drawing her close to him.

Athena surrendered willingly to his kiss, a deep joy filling her.

Life with Nick might not be easy but together they would weather the storms. He was the calm beyond the reef, the safe haven she had always longed for. She had come home.